The millennium is near. . . .

The battle is coming. The lines are being drawn. The new Night People are more ruthless and bloodthirsty than ever before, and they're getting ready to destroy the human world. But the light has its champions, too. Four children have been born, four Wild Powers who can stop the darkness from winning . . . if they and their soulmates can survive.

Romantic horror reaches new heights in these tales of terror and forbidden love.

L.J.SMITH

NIGHT WORLD®

Huntress

AN ARCHWAY PAPERBACK
Published by POCKET BOOKS
New York London Toronto Sydney Tokyo Singapore

This book is a work of fiction. Names, characters, places and incidents are products of the author's imagination or are used fictitiously. Any resemblance to actual events or locales or persons, living or dead, is entirely coincidental.

AN ARCHWAY PAPERBACK *Original*

An Archway Paperback published by
POCKET BOOKS, a division of Simon & Schuster Inc.
1230 Avenue of the Americas, New York, NY 10020

Copyright © 1997 by Lisa J. Smith

ISBN: 0-671-01475-7

First Archway Paperback printing September 1997

10 9 8 7 6 5 4 3 2

NIGHT WORLD is a registered trademark of Lisa J. Smith

AN ARCHWAY PAPERBACK and colophon are registered trademarks of Simon & Schuster Inc.

Cover art by Sanjulian

Printed in the U.S.A.

IL 7+

For Brian Nelson and Justin Lauffenburger

The Night World . . . love was never so scary.

The Night World isn't a place. It's all around us. It's a secret society of vampires, werewolves, witches, and other creatures of darkness that live among us. They're beautiful and deadly and irresistible to humans. Your high school teacher could be one, and so could your boyfriend.

The Night World laws say it's okay to hunt humans. It's okay to toy with their hearts, it's even okay to kill them. There are only two things you can't do with them.

1) Never let them find out that the Night World exists.
2) Never fall in love with one of them.

These are stories about what happens when the rules get broken.

Huntress

CHAPTER

1

It's simple," Jez said on the night of the last hunt of her life. "You run. We chase. If we catch you, you die. We'll give you three minutes head start."

The skinhead gang leader in front of her didn't move. He had a pasty face and shark eyes. He was standing tensely, trying to look tough, but Jez could see the little quiver in his leg muscles.

Jez flashed him a smile.

"Pick a weapon," she said. Her toe nudged the pile at her feet. There was a lot of stuff there— guns, knives, baseball bats, even a few spears. "Hey, take *more* than one. Take as many as you want. My treat."

There was a stifled giggle from behind her and Jez made a sharp gesture to stop it. Then there was silence. The two gangs stood facing each other, six skinhead thugs on one side and Jez's gang on the other. Except that Jez's people weren't exactly normal gang members.

The skinhead leader's eyes shifted to the pile. Then he made a sudden lunge and came up with something in his hand.

A gun, of course. They always picked guns. This particular gun was the kind it was illegal to buy in California these days, a large caliber semiautomatic assault weapon. The skinhead whipped it up and held it pointed straight at Jez.

Jez threw back her head and laughed.

Everyone was staring at her—and that was fine. She looked great and she knew it.

Hands on her hips, red hair tumbling over her shoulders and down her back, fine-boned face tipped to the sky—yeah, she looked good. Tall and proud and fierce . . . and very beautiful. She was Jez Redfern, the huntress.

She lowered her chin and fixed the gang leader with eyes that were neither silver nor blue but some color in between. A color he never could have seen before, because no human had eyes like that.

He didn't get the clue. He didn't seem like the brightest.

"Chase this," he said, and he fired the gun.

Jez moved at the last instant. Not that metal through the chest would have seriously hurt her, but it might have knocked her backward and she didn't want that. She'd just taken over the leadership of the gang from Morgead, and she didn't want to show any weakness.

The bullet passed through her left arm. There was a little explosion of blood and a sharp flash of pain as it fractured the bone before passing on through. Jez narrowed her eyes, but held on to her smile.

Then she glanced down at her arm and lost the smile, hissing. She hadn't considered the damage to her sleeve. Now there was a bloody hole in it. Why didn't she ever think about these things?

"Do you know how much leather costs? Do you know how much a North Beach jacket costs?" She advanced on the skinhead leader.

He was blinking and hyperventilating. Trying to figure out how she'd moved so fast and why she wasn't yelling in agony. He aimed the gun and fired again. And again, each time more wildly.

Jez dodged. She didn't want any more holes. The flesh of her arm was already healing, closing up and smoothing over. Too bad her jacket couldn't do the same. She reached the skinhead without getting hit again and grabbed him by the front of his green and black Air Force flight jacket. She lifted him, one handed, until the steel toes of his Doc Marten boots just cleared the ground.

"You better run, boy," she said. Then she threw him.

He sailed through the air a remarkable distance and bounced off a tree. He scrambled up, his eyes showing white with terror, his chest heaving. He looked at her, looked at his gang, then turned and started running through the redwoods.

The other gang members stared after him for a

moment before diving for the weapons pile. Jez watched them, frowning. They'd just seen how effective bullets were against people like her, but they still went for the guns, passing by perfectly good split-bamboo knives, yew arrows, and a gorgeous snakewood walking stick.

And then things were noisy for a while as the skinheads came up from the pile and started firing. Jez's gang dodged easily, but an exasperated voice sounded in Jez's head.

Can we go after them now? *Or do you want to show off some more?*

She flicked a glance behind her. Morgead Blackthorn was seventeen, a year older than she, and her worst enemy. He was conceited, hotheaded, stubborn, and power-hungry—and it didn't help that he was always saying she was all those things, too.

"I told them three minutes," she said out loud. "You want me to break my word?" And for that instant, while she was snarling at him, she forgot to keep track of bullets.

The next thing she knew Morgead was knocking her backward. He was lying on top of her. Something whizzed over both of them and hit a tree, spraying bark.

Morgead's gem-green eyes glared down into hers. "But . . . they're . . . not . . . running," he said with exaggerated patience. "In case you hadn't noticed."

He was too close. His hands were on either side of her head. His weight was on her. Jez kicked him off, furious with him and appalled at herself.

"This is *my* game. *I* thought of it. We play it my way!" she yelled.

The skinheads were scattering anyway. They'd finally realized that shooting was pointless. They were running, crashing through the sword fern.

"Okay, now!" Jez said. "But the leader's mine."

There was a chorus of shouts and hunting calls from her gang. Val, the biggest and always the most impatient, dashed off first, yelling something like "Yeeeeeehaw." Then Thistle and Raven went, the slight blond and the tall dark girl sticking together as always. Pierce hung back, staring with his cold eyes at a tree, waiting to give his prey the illusion of escaping.

Jez didn't look to see what Morgead was doing. Why should she care?

She started off in the direction the skinhead leader had taken. But she didn't exactly take his path. She went through the trees, jumping from one redwood to another. The giant sequoias were the best; they had the thickest branches, although the wartlike bulges called burls on the coastal redwoods were good landing places, too. Jez jumped and grabbed and jumped again, occasionally doing acrobatic flips when she caught a branch just for the fun of it.

She loved Muir Woods. Even though all the wood around her was deadly—or maybe because it was. She liked taking risks. And the place was beautiful: the cathedral silence, the mossy greenness, the resinous smell.

Last week they'd hunted seven gang members

through Golden Gate Park. It had been enjoyable, but not really private, and they couldn't let the humans fight back much. Gunshots in the park would attract attention. Muir Woods had been Jez's idea—they could kidnap the gang members and bring them here where nobody would disturb them. They would give them weapons. It would be a real hunt, with real danger.

Jez squatted on a branch to catch her breath. There just wasn't enough real danger in the world, she thought. Not like the old days, when there were still vampire hunters left in the Bay Area. Jez's parents had been killed by vampire hunters. But now that they'd all been eliminated, there wasn't anything really scary anymore. . . .

She froze. There was an almost inaudible crunching in the pine needles ahead of her. Instantly she was on the move again, leaping fearlessly off the branch into space, landing on the spongy pine-needle carpet with her knees bent. She turned and stood face-to-face with the skinhead.

"Hey there," she said.

CHAPTER

2

The skinhead's face was contorted, his eyes huge. He stared at her, breathing hard like a hurt animal.

"I know," Jez said. "You ran fast. You can't figure out how I ran faster."

"You're—not—human," the skinhead panted. Except that he threw in a lot of other words, the kind humans liked to use when they were upset.

"You guessed," Jez said cheerfully, ignoring the obscenities. "You're not as dumb as you look."

"What—the hell—are you?"

"Death." Jez smiled at him. "Are you going to fight? I hope so."

He fumbled the gun up again. His hands were shaking so hard he could scarcely aim it.

"I think you're out of ammo," Jez said. "But anyway a branch would be better. You want me to break one off for you?"

He pulled the trigger. The gun just clicked. He looked at it.

Jez smiled at him, showing her teeth.

She could feel them grow as she went into feeding mode. Her canines lengthening and curving until they were as sharp and delicate and translucent as a cat's. She liked the feel of them lightly indenting her lower lip as she half-opened her mouth.

That wasn't the only change. She knew that her eyes were turning to liquid silver and her lips were getting redder and fuller as blood flowed into them in anticipation of feeding. Her whole body was taking on an indefinable charge of energy.

The skinhead watched as she became more and more beautiful, more and more inhuman. And then he seemed to fold in on himself. With his back against a tree, he slid down until he was sitting on the ground in the middle of some pale brown oyster fungus. He was staring straight ahead.

Jez's gaze was drawn to the double lightning bolt tattooed on his neck. Right . . . there, she thought. The skin seemed reasonably clean, and the smell of blood was enticing. It was running there, rich with adrenaline, in blue veins just under the surface. She was almost intoxicated just thinking about tapping it.

Fear was good; it added that extra spice to the taste. Like Sweetarts. This was going to be good. . . .

Then she heard a soft broken sound.

The skinhead was crying.

Not loud bawling. Not blubbering and begging. Just crying like a kid, slow tears trickling down his cheeks as he shook.

"I thought better of you," Jez said. She shook her hair out, tossed it in contempt. But something inside her seemed to tighten.

He didn't say anything. He just stared at her—no, *through* her—and cried. Jez knew what he was seeing. His own death.

"Oh, come on," Jez said. "So you don't want to die. Who does? But you've killed people before. Your gang killed that guy Juan last week. You can dish it out, but you can't take it."

He still didn't say anything. He wasn't pointing the gun at her anymore; he was clutching it with both hands to his chest as if it were a teddy bear or something. Or maybe as if he were going to kill himself to get away from her. The muzzle of the gun was under his chin.

The thing inside Jez tightened more. Tightened and twisted until she couldn't breathe. What was wrong with her? He was just a human, and a human of the worst kind. He *deserved* to die, and not just because she was hungry.

But the sound of that crying . . . It seemed to pull at her. She had a feeling almost of déjà vu, as if this had all happened before—but it *hadn't*. She knew it hadn't.

The skinhead spoke at last. "Do it quick," he whispered.

And Jez's mind was thrown into chaos.

With just those words she was suddenly not in the forest anymore. She was falling into nothingness, whirling and spinning, with nothing to grab hold of. She saw pictures in bright, disjointed flashes. Nothing made sense; she was plunging in darkness with scenes unreeling before her helpless eyes.

"Do it quickly," somebody whispered. A flash and Jez saw who: a woman with dark red hair and delicate, bony shoulders. She had a face like a medieval princess. "I won't fight you," the woman said. "Kill me. But let my daughter live."

Mother . . .

These were her memories.

She wanted to see more of her mother—she didn't have any conscious memory of the woman who'd given birth to her. But instead there was another flash. A little girl was huddled in a corner, shaking. The child had flame-bright hair and eyes that were neither silver nor blue. And she was so frightened . . .

Another flash. A tall man running to the child. Turning around, standing in front of her. "Leave her alone! It's not her fault. She doesn't have to die!"

Daddy.

Her parents, who'd been killed when she was four. Executed by vampire hunters. . . .

Another flash and she saw fighting. Blood. Dark figures struggling with her mother and father. And screaming that wouldn't quite resolve into words.

And then one of the dark figures picked up the little girl in the corner and held her up high . . . and Jez saw that he had fangs. He wasn't a vampire hunter; he was a vampire.

And the little girl, whose mouth was open in a wail, had none.

All at once, Jez could understand the screaming. "Kill her! Kill the human! Kill the freak!"

They were screaming it about *her*.

Jez came back to herself. She was in Muir Woods, kneeling in the ferns and moss, with the skinhead cowering in front of her. Everything was the same . . . but everything was different. She felt dazed and terrified.

What did it *mean*?

It was just some bizarre hallucination. It had to be. She knew how her parents had died. Her mother had been murdered outright by the vampire hunters. Her father had been mortally wounded, but he'd managed to carry the four-year-old Jez to his brother's house before he died. Uncle Bracken had raised her, and he'd told her the story over and over.

But that screaming . . .

It didn't mean anything. It *couldn't*. She was Jez Redfern, more of a vampire than anyone, even Morgead. Of all the lamia, the vampires who could have children, her family was the most important. Her uncle Bracken was a vampire, and so was his father, and his father's father, all the way back to Hunter Redfern.

But her mother . . .

What did she know about her mother's family? Nothing. Uncle Bracken always just said that they'd come from the East Coast.

Something inside Jez was trembling. She didn't want to frame the next question, but the words came into her mind anyway, blunt and inescapable.

What if her mother had been human?

That would make Jez . . .

No. It wasn't possible. It wasn't just that Night World law forbade vampires to fall in love with humans. It was that there was no such thing as a vampire-human hybrid. It couldn't be *done;* it had never been done in twenty thousand years. Anybody like that would be a freak. . . .

The trembling inside her was getting worse.

She stood up slowly and only vaguely noticed when the skinhead made a sound of fear. She couldn't focus on him. She was staring between the redwood trees.

If it were true . . . it *couldn't* be true, but if it were true . . . she would have to leave everything. Uncle Bracken. The gang.

And Morgead. She'd have to leave Morgead. For some reason that made her throat close convulsively.

And she would go . . . where? What kind of a place was there for a half-human half-vampire freak?

Nowhere in the Night World. That was certain. The Night People would have to kill any creature like that.

The skinhead made another sound, a little whimper. Jez blinked and looked at him.

It couldn't be true, but all of a sudden she didn't care about killing him anymore. In fact, she had a feeling like slow horror creeping over her, as if something in her brain was tallying up all the humans she'd hurt and killed over the years. Something was taking over her legs, making her knees rubbery. Something was crushing her chest, making her feel as if she were going to be sick.

"Get out of here," she whispered to the skinhead.

He shut his eyes. When he spoke it was in a kind of moan. "You'll just chase me."

"No." But she understood his fear. She was a huntress. She'd chased so many people. So many humans . . .

Jez shuddered violently and shut her eyes. It was as if she had suddenly seen herself in a mirror and the image was unbearable. It wasn't Jez the proud and fierce and beautiful. It was Jez the murderer.

I have to stop the others.

The telepathic call she sent out was almost a scream. *Everybody! This is Jez. Come to me, right now! Drop what you're doing and come!*

She knew they'd obey—they were her gang, after all. But none of them except Morgead had enough telepathic power to answer across the distance.

What's wrong? he said.

Jez stood very still. She couldn't tell him the truth. Morgead hated humans. If he even knew what she suspected . . . the way he would look at her . . .

He would be sickened. Not to mention that he'd undoubtedly have to kill her.

I'll explain later, she told him, feeling numb. *I just found out—that it's not safe to feed here.*

Then she cut the telepathic link short. She was afraid he'd sense too much of what was going on inside her.

She stood with her arms wrapped around herself, staring between the trees. Then she glanced at the skinhead, who was still huddled in the sword fern.

There was one last thing she had to do with him.

Ignoring his wild flinching, she stretched out her hand. Touched him, once, on the forehead with an extended finger. A gentle, precise contact.

"Remember . . . nothing," she said. "Now go."

She felt the power flow out of her, wrapping itself around the skinhead's brain, changing its chemistry, rearranging his thoughts. It was something she was very good at.

The skinhead's eyes went blank. Jez didn't watch him as he began to crawl away.

All she could think of now was getting to Uncle Bracken. He would answer her questions; he would explain. He would prove to her that none of it was true.

He'd make everything all right.

CHAPTER

3

Jez burst through the door and turned immediately into the small library off the front hall. Her uncle was sitting there at his desk, surrounded by built-in bookcases. He looked up in surprise.

"Uncle Bracken, who was my mother? How did my parents die?" It all came out in a single rush of breath. And then Jez wanted to say, "Tell me the truth," but instead she heard herself saying wildly, "Tell me it's not true. It's not possible, is it? Uncle Bracken, I'm so scared."

Her uncle stared at her for a moment. There was shock and despair in his face. Then he bent his head and shut his eyes.

"But how is it possible?" Jez whispered. "How am I here?" It was hours later. Dawn was tinting the window. She was sitting on the floor, back against a bookcase, where she'd collapsed, staring emptily into the distance.

"You mean, how can a vampire-human halfbreed exist? I don't know. Your parents never knew. They never expected to have children." Uncle Bracken ran both hands through his hair, head down. "They didn't even realize you could live as a vampire. Your father brought you to me because he was dying and I was the only person he could trust. He knew I wouldn't turn you over to the Night World elders."

"Maybe you should have," Jez whispered.

Uncle Bracken went on as if he hadn't heard her. "You lived without blood then. You looked like a human child. I don't know what made me try to see if you could learn how to feed. I brought you a rabbit and bit it for you and let you smell the blood." He gave a short laugh of reminiscence. "And your little teeth sharpened right up and you knew what to do. That was when I knew you were a true Redfern."

"But I'm not." Jez heard the words as if someone else was speaking them from a distance. "I'm not even a Night Person. I'm vermin."

Uncle Bracken let go of his hair and looked at her. His eyes, normally the same silvery-blue as Jez's, were burning with a pure silver flame. "Your mother was a good woman," he said harshly. "Your father gave up everything to be with her. She wasn't vermin."

Jez looked away, but she wasn't ashamed. She

was numb. She felt nothing except a vast emptiness inside her, stretching infinitely in all directions.

And that was good. She never wanted to feel again. Everything she'd felt in her life—everything she could remember—had been a lie.

She wasn't a huntress, a predator fulfilling her place in the scheme of things by chasing down her lawful prey. She was a murderer. She was a monster.

"I can't stay here anymore," she said.

Uncle Bracken winced. "Where will you go?"

"I don't know."

He let out his breath and spoke slowly and sadly. "I have an idea."

CHAPTER

4

Rule Number One of living with humans. Always wash the blood off before coming in the house.

Jez stood at the outdoor faucet, icy-cold water splashing over her hands. She was scrubbing—carefully—a long, slim dagger made of split bamboo, with a cutting edge as sharp as glass. When it was clean, she slipped it into her right knee-high boot. Then she daubed water over several stains on her T-shirt and jeans and scrubbed them with a fingernail. Finally she whipped out a pocket mirror and examined her face critically.

The girl who looked back didn't much resemble the wild, laughing huntress who had leaped from tree to tree in Muir Woods. Oh, the features were the same; the height of cheekbone, the curve of chin. They had even fined out a bit because she was a year older. The red flag of hair was the same, too, although now it was pulled back in an attempt to tame its fiery disorder. The difference was in the expression, which was sadder and wiser than Jez had ever imagined she could be, and in the eyes.

The eyes weren't as silvery as they had been, not as dangerously beautiful. But that was only to be expected. She had discovered that she didn't need to drink blood as long as she didn't use her vampire powers. Human food kept her alive—and made her look more human.

One other thing about the eyes. They were scarily vulnerable, even to Jez. No matter how she tried to make them hard and menacing, they had the wounded look of a deer that knows it's going to die and accepts it. Sometimes she wondered if that was an omen.

Well. No blood on her face. She shoved the mirror back in her pocket. She was mostly presentable, if extremely late for dinner. She turned the faucet off and headed for the back door of the low, sweeping ranch house.

Everyone looked up as she came in.

The family was in the kitchen, eating at the oak table with the white trim, under the bright fluorescent light. The TV was blaring cheerfully from the family room. Uncle Jim, her mother's brother, was munching tacos and leafing through the mail. He had red hair darker than Jez's and a long face that looked almost as medieval as Jez's mother's had. He was usually off in a gentle, worried dream somewhere. Now he waved an envelope at Jez and gazed at her reproachfully, but he couldn't say anything because his mouth was full.

Aunt Nanami was on the phone, drinking a diet Coke. She was small, with dark shiny hair and eyes that turned to crescents when she smiled. She opened her mouth and frowned at Jez, but couldn't say anything, either.

Ricky, who was ten, had carroty hair and expressive eyebrows. He gave Jez a big smile that showed chewed-up taco in his mouth and said, "Hi!"

Jez smiled back. No matter what she did, Ricky was there for her.

Claire, who was Jez's age, was sitting primly, eating bits of taco with her fork. She looked like a smaller version of Aunt Nan, but with a very sour expression.

"Where have you *been?*" she said. "We waited dinner almost an hour for you and you never even called."

"Sorry," Jez said, looking at all of them. It was such an incredibly normal family scene, so completely typical, and it struck her to the heart.

It was over a year since she had walked out of the Night World to find these people, her mother's relatives. It was eleven and a half months since Uncle Jim had taken her in, not knowing anything about her except that she was his orphaned niece and that her father's family couldn't handle her anymore and had given up on her. All these months, she had lived with the Goddard family—and she still didn't fit in.

She could look human, she could act human, but she couldn't *be* human.

Just as Uncle Jim swallowed and got his mouth clear to speak to her, she said, "I'm not hungry. I think I'll just go do my homework."

Uncle Jim called, "Wait a minute," after her, but it was Claire who slammed down her napkin and actually followed Jez through the hall to the other side of the house.

"What do you *mean*, 'Sorry'? You do this every day. You're always disappearing; half the time you stay out until after midnight, and then you don't even have an explanation."

"Yeah, I know, Claire." Jez answered without looking back. "I'll try to do better."

"You say that every time. And every time it's exactly the same. Don't you realize that my parents worry about you? Don't you even care?"

"Yes, I care, Claire."

"You don't act like it. You act like rules don't apply to you. And you say sorry, but you're just going to do it again."

Jez had to keep herself from turning around and snapping at her cousin. She liked everyone else in the family, but Claire was a royal pain.

Worse, she was a *shrewd* royal pain. And she was right; Jez was going to do it again, and there was no way she could explain.

The thing was, vampire hunters have to keep weird hours.

When you're on the trail of a vampire-and-shapeshifter killing team, as Jez had been this evening, chasing them through the slums of Oakland, trying to get them cornered in some crack house where there aren't little kids to get hurt, you don't think about missing dinner. You don't stop in the middle of staking the undead to phone home.

Maybe I shouldn't have become a vampire hunter, Jez thought. But it's a little late to change now, and *somebody's* got to protect these stupid— these innocent humans from the Night World.

Oh, well.

She'd reached the door of her bedroom. Instead of yelling at her cousin, she simply half turned and said, "Why don't you go work on your Web page, Claire?" Then she opened the door and glanced inside.

And froze.

Her room, which she had left in military neatness, was a shambles. The window was wide open. Papers and clothes were scattered across the floor. And there was a very large ghoul standing at the foot of the bed.

The ghoul opened its mouth menacingly at Jez.

"Oh, very funny," Claire was saying, right behind her. "Maybe I should help you with your homework. I hear you're not doing so great in chemistry—"

Jez moved fast, stepping nimbly inside the door and slamming it in Claire's face, pressing the little knob in the handle to lock it.

"Hey!" Now Claire sounded *really* mad. "That's rude!"

"Uh, sorry, Claire!" Jez faced the ghoul. What was it *doing* here? If it had followed her home, she was in bad trouble. That meant the Night World knew where she was. "You know, Claire, I think I really need to be alone for a little while—I can't talk *and* do my homework." She took a step toward the creature, watching its reaction.

Ghouls were semi-vampires. They were what happened to a human who was bled out but didn't get quite enough vampire blood in exchange to become a true vampire. They were undead but rotting. They had very little mind, and only one idea in the world: to drink blood, which they usually did by eating as much of a human body as possible. They liked hearts.

This ghoul was a new one, about two weeks dead. It was male and looked as if it had been a body-builder, although by now it wasn't so much buff as puffed. Its body was swollen with the gas of decomposition. Its tongue and eyes were protruding, its cheeks were chipmunklike, and bloody fluid was leaking from its nose.

And of course it didn't smell good.

As Jez edged closer, she suddenly realized that the ghoul wasn't alone. She could now see around the foot of the bed, and there was a boy lying on the carpet, apparently unconscious. The boy had light hair and rumpled clothes, but Jez couldn't see his face. The ghoul was stooping over him, reaching for him with sausage-shaped fingers.

"I don't think so," Jez told it softly. She could feel a dangerous smile settling on her face. She reached into her right boot and pulled out the dagger.

"What did you say?" Claire shouted from the other side of the door.

"Nothing, Claire. Just getting out my homework." Jez jumped onto the bed. The ghoul was very big— she needed all the height she could get.

The ghoul turned to face her, its lackluster bug-eyes on the dagger. It made a little hissing sound around its swollen tongue. Fortunately that was all the noise it could make.

Claire was rattling the door. "Did you *lock* this? What are you doing in there?"

"Just studying, Claire. Go away." Jez snapped a foot toward the ghoul, catching it under the chin. She needed to stun it and stake it fast. Ghouls weren't smart, but like the Energizer Bunny they kept going and going. This one could eat the entire Goddard family tonight and still be hungry at dawn.

The ghoul hit the wall opposite the bed. Jez jumped down, putting herself between it and the boy on the floor.

"What was that *noise?*" Claire yelled.

"I dropped a book."

The ghoul swung. Jez ducked. There were giant blisters on its arms, the brownish color of old blood.

It rushed her, trying to slam her against the chest of drawers. Jez flung herself backward, but she didn't have much room to maneuver. It caught her in the stomach with an elbow, a jarring blow.

Jez wouldn't let herself double over. She twisted and helped the ghoul in the direction it was already going, giving it impetus with her foot. It smacked into the window seat, facedown.

"What is going on in there?"

"Just looking for something." Jez moved before the ghoul could recover, jumping to straddle its legs. She grabbed its hair—not a good idea; it came off in clumps in her hand. Kneeling on it to keep it still, she raised the slim bamboo knife high and brought it down hard.

There was a puncturing sound and a terrible smell. The knife had penetrated just under the shoulder blade, six inches into the heart.

The ghoul convulsed once and stopped moving.

Claire's voice came piercingly from behind the closed door. "Mom! She's *doing* something in there!"

Then Aunt Nan's voice: "Jez, are you all right?"

Jez stood, pulling her bamboo dagger out, wiping it on the ghoul's shirt. "I'm just having a little trouble finding a ruler. . . ." The ghoul was in a perfect position. She put her arms around its waist, ignoring the feeling of skin slipping loose under her fingers, and heaved it up onto the window seat. There weren't many human girls who could have picked up almost two hundred pounds of dead weight, and even Jez ended up a little breathless. She gave the ghoul a shove, rolling it over until it reached the open window, then she stuffed and maneuvered it out. It fell heavily into a bed of impatiens, squashing the flowers.

Good. She'd haul it away later tonight and dispose of it.

Jez caught her breath, brushed off her hands, and closed the window. She drew the curtains shut, then turned. The fair-haired boy was lying perfectly still. Jez touched his back gently, saw that he was breathing.

The door rattled and Claire's voice rose hysterically. "Mom, do you smell that *smell?*"

Aunt Nan called, "Jez!"

"Coming!" Jez glanced around the room. She needed something . . . there. The bed.

Grabbing a handful of material near the head of the bed, she flipped comforter, blankets and sheets over so they trailed off the foot, completely covering the boy. She tossed a couple of pillows on top of the pile for good measure, then grabbed a ruler off the desk. Then she opened the door, leaned against the doorframe casually, and summoned her brightest smile.

"Sorry about that," she said. "What can I do for you?"

Claire and Aunt Nan just stared at her.

Claire looked like a rumpled, angry kitten. The fine dark hair that framed her face was ruffled; she was breathing hard, and her almond-shaped eyes were flashing sparks. Aunt Nan looked more worried and dismayed.

"Are you okay?" she said, leaning in slightly to try and get a look at Jez's room. "We heard a lot of noise."

And you'd have heard more earlier if you hadn't been watching TV. "I'm fine. I'm great. You know how it is when you can't find something." Jez lifted the ruler. Then she stepped back and opened the door farther.

Aunt Nan's eyes widened as she took in the mess. "Jez . . . this does not happen when you can't find a ruler. This looks like *Claire's* room."

Claire made a choked sound of indignation. "It does not. My room's *never* been this bad. And what's that *smell?*" She slipped by Aunt Nan and advanced on Jez, who sidestepped to keep her from getting to the pile of blankets.

Claire stopped dead anyway, her face wrinkling. She put a hand to cover her nose and mouth. "It's *you,*" she said, pointing at Jez. "*You* smell like that."

"Sorry." It was true; what with all the contact she'd had with the ghoul, and the dirty knife in her boot, she was pretty ripe. "I think I stepped in something on the way home."

"I didn't smell anything when you came in," Claire said suspiciously.

"And that's another thing," Aunt Nan said. She had been glancing around the room, but there was nothing suspicious to see except the unusual clutter—the curtains hung motionless over the shut window; the pile of bedding on the floor was still. Now she turned to face Jez again. "You didn't call to say you were going to miss dinner again. I need to know where you go after school, Jez. I need to know when you're going to be out late. It's common courtesy."

"I know. I'll remember next time. I really will." Jez said it as sincerely as possible, and in a tone she hoped would close the subject. She needed to get rid of these people and look at the boy under the blankets. He might be seriously hurt.

Aunt Nan was nodding. "You'd better. And you'd better take a shower before you do anything else. Throw your clothes in the laundry room; I'll put them in the wash." She made as if to kiss Jez on the cheek, but stopped, wrinkled her nose, and then just nodded again at her.

"And that's it? That's all?" Claire was looking at her mother in disbelief. "Mom, she's *up* to something, can't you see that? She comes in late, smelling like dead skunk and sewage and I don't know what, and then she locks herself in and bangs around and lies, and all you're going to say is 'Don't do it again'? She gets away with *everything* around here—"

"Claire, quit it. She said she was sorry. I'm sure she won't let it happen again."

"If *I* did something like that you'd skin me, but, no, if Jez does it, it must be okay. Well, I'll tell you something else. She cut school today. She left before sixth period."

"Is that true, Jez?" a new voice asked. Uncle Jim was standing in the doorway, pulling at his chin with long fingers. He looked sad.

It was true. Jez had left early to set up a trap for the vampire and shapeshifter. She looked at her uncle and made a regretful motion with her head and shoulders.

"Jez, you just can't *do* that. I'm trying to be reasonable, but this is only the second week of school.

You can't start this kind of behavior again. It can't be like last year." He thought. "From now on, you leave your motorcycle at home. You drive to school and back with Claire, in the Audi."

Jez nodded. "Okay, Uncle Jim," she said out loud. Now go away, she added silently. Thin curls of anxiety were churning in her stomach.

"Thank you." He smiled at her.

"See?" Claire jumped in, her voice hitting a note to shatter glass. "This is just what I'm talking about! You never yell at her, either! Is it because you're afraid she'll run away, like she did from her dad's relatives? So everybody has to walk on eggshells around her because otherwise she'll just take off—"

"Okay, that's it. I'm not listening to any more of this." Aunt Nan waved a hand at Claire, then turned around to shoo Uncle Jim out of her path. "I'm going to clean up the dinner table. If you two want to fight, do it quietly."

"No, it's better if they do their homework," Uncle Jim said, moving slowly. "Both of you, do your homework, okay?" He looked at Jez in a way that was probably meant to be commanding, but came out wistful. "And tomorrow come home on time."

Jez nodded. Then both adults were gone, but Claire was staring after them. Jez couldn't be sure, but she thought there were tears in her eyes.

Jez felt a pang. Of course, Claire was dead on about the leeway Aunt Nan and Uncle Jim gave her. And of course, it *wasn't* fair to Claire.

I should say something to her. Poor little thing. She really feels bad. . . .

But before she could open her mouth, Claire whirled around. The eyes that had been wet a moment ago were flashing.

"You just wait," she said. "They don't see through you, but *I* do. You're up to something, and I'm going to find out what it is. *And don't think I can't do it.*"

She turned and stalked out the door.

Jez stood for an instant, speechless, then she blinked and closed the door. She locked it. And then for the first time since she'd seen the ghoul, she allowed herself to let out a long breath.

That had been close. And Claire was serious, which was going to be a problem. But Jez didn't have time to think about it now.

She turned the clock radio on her nightstand to a rock station. A loud one. Then she flipped the covers off the foot of the bed and knelt.

The boy was lying facedown, with one arm stretched over his head. Jez couldn't see any blood. She took his shoulder and carefully rolled him over.

And stopped breathing.

"Hugh."

CHAPTER

5

The boy's light hair was longish, falling over his forehead in disarray. He had a nice face, serious, but with an unexpected dimple in his chin that gave him a slightly mischievous look. His body was nicely muscled but compact; standing, Jez knew, he'd be no taller than she. There was a large bump coming up on his forehead, just under the falling hair. The ghoul had probably slammed him against something.

Jez jumped up and got a blue plastic cup full of water from her nightstand. She grabbed a clean T-shirt from the floor and dipped it into the water, then she gently brushed back the hair from the boy's forehead.

It was silky under her fingers. Even softer than she would have thought. Jez kept her face expressionless and began to wipe his face with the damp cloth.

He didn't stir. Jez's heart, which was already thumping distinctly, speeded up. She took a deep breath and kept wiping.

Finally, although it probably didn't have anything to do with the water, the boy's dark eyelashes moved. He coughed, breathed, blinked, and looked at her.

Relief spread through Jez. "Don't try to sit up yet."

"That's what they all say," he agreed, and sat up. He put a hand to his head and groaned. Jez steadied him.

"I'm fine," he said. "Just tell the room to stop moving." He looked around the room, blinked again and suddenly seemed to focus. He grabbed her arm, his eyes wide. "Something followed me—"

"A ghoul. It's dead."

He let out his breath. Then he smiled wryly. "You saved my life."

"And I don't even charge," Jez said, embarrassed.

"No, I mean it." His smile faded and he looked straight at her. "Thank you."

Jez could feel heat trying to rise to her face, and she had a hard time holding his gaze. His eyes were gray and so intense—fathomless. Her skin was tingling.

She looked away and said evenly, "We should get you to a hospital. You might have a concussion."

"No. I'm okay. Let me just see if I can stand up."

When she opened her mouth to protest, he added, "Jez, you don't know why I'm here. It can't wait."

He was right; Jez had been so intent on getting him conscious that she hadn't even wondered what he was doing here. She looked at him for a moment, then nodded. She helped him up, and let go of his arm when she saw he could stand without falling over.

"See, I'm fine." He took a few steps, then made a circuit of the room, loosening his muscles. Jez watched him narrowly, ready to grab him if he fell. But he walked steadily except for a slight limp.

And that wasn't from his encounter with the ghoul tonight, Jez knew. He'd had the limp from childhood, from when the werewolves took his family.

How he'd been able to get over that and join Circle Daybreak, Jez would never know.

He'd lost his parents almost as young as she had. He'd lost his two sisters and his brother, too. His entire family had been on a camping trip at Lake Tahoe, when in the middle of the night they'd been attacked by a pack of werewolves. Renegade 'wolves, hunting illegally because Night World law wouldn't let them kill as often as they liked.

Just like Jez's old gang.

The 'wolves had ripped through the Davis family's tents and killed the humans, one, two, three. Easy as that. The only one they left alive was seven-year-old Hugh, because he was too little to have much meat on his body. They had just settled down to eat the hearts and livers of their victims, when suddenly the one too little to be worth eating was dashing at them with a homemade torch constructed of kerosene-soaked underwear wrapped around a stick. He was also waving a silver cross on a chain the werewolves had torn from his sister's neck.

Two things werewolves don't like: silver and fire. The little boy was attacking with both. The 'wolves decided to kill him.

Slowly.

They almost did it. They managed to chew one of his legs almost off before a park ranger arrived, attracted by the spreading fire from the dropped torch.

The ranger had a gun, and the fire was getting out of control. The 'wolves left.

Hugh almost died of blood loss on the way to the hospital.

But he was a tough kid. And a very smart one. He didn't even try to explain to anybody what he'd been doing with the silver necklace. He knew they would never believe him if he said he'd suddenly remembered a bunch of past lives, including one where he'd seen a werewolf killed.

Hugh Davis was an Old Soul.

And a *wakened* Old Soul, which was even more rare. It scared Jez a little. He was human and she was from the Night World, but she didn't pretend to understand the magic that brought some humans back again and again, reincarnating them in new bodies. Letting them remember all their past lifetimes, making them smarter and more clearheaded every time they were born.

In Hugh's case, also gentler every time. In spite of the attack on his family, when he got out of the hospital the first thing he did was try to find some Night People. He knew they weren't all bad. He knew some of them would help him stop the werewolves from hurting anyone else.

Fortunately, the first people he found were from Circle Daybreak.

Circles were witch organizations, but Circle Daybreak was for humans and vampires and shapeshifters and werewolves, too. It was an underground society, as secret within the Night World as the Night World was secret within the human world. It went against the most basic tenets of Night World law: that humans were not to be told about the Night World, and that Night People shouldn't fall in love with humans. Circle Daybreak was fighting to unite everybody, to stop the killings, and to bring peace between the races.

Jez wished them luck.

She suddenly realized that Hugh had stopped walking and was looking at her. She blinked and focused, furious with herself for her slip in concentration. As a huntress—of vampires or anything else—you stayed alert all the time, or you were dead.

"You were miles away," Hugh said softly. His gray eyes were calm but intense as always. That look Old Souls get when they're reading you, Jez thought.

She said, "Sorry. Um, do you want some ice for that bump?"

"No, I like it. I'm thinking of getting one on the other side, to match." He sat on the bed, serious again. "Really, I've got some stuff to explain to you, and it's going to take a while."

Jez didn't sit. "Hugh, I think you need it. And I need to take a shower or my aunt will get suspicious about what I'm doing in here for so long. Besides, the smell is driving me crazy." Although she couldn't use her vampire powers without bringing on the bloodlust, her senses were still much more acute than a human's.

"Eau de Ghoul? And I was just starting to enjoy it." Hugh nodded at her, switching from gentle humor to gentle gravity as always. "You need to do what will keep your cover here. I shouldn't be so impatient."

Jez took the fastest shower of her life, then dressed in clean clothes she'd brought to the bathroom. As she returned carrying a glassful of ice from the kitchen and a washcloth, she saw that Claire's bedroom door was ajar and Claire was watching her narrowly.

Jez raised the glass in a mock toast, and slipped into her own bedroom.

"Here." She made an ice pack and handed it to Hugh. He accepted it docilely. "Now, what is it that's so urgent? And how come you're so popular with ghouls all of a sudden?"

Instead of answering, Hugh looked into a middle distance. He was bracing himself for something. Finally he lowered the ice pack and looked straight at her.

"You know I care about you. If anything happened to you, I don't know what I'd do. And if anything happened because of *me* . . ." He shook his head.

Jez told her heart to get down where it belonged. It was pounding in her throat, choking her. She kept her voice flat as she said, "Thanks."

Something like hurt flashed in his eyes and was gone instantly. "You don't think I mean it."

Jez still spoke flatly, in a clipped, hurried voice. She wasn't good at talking about emotional stuff. "Hugh, look. You were my first human friend. When I came to live here, nobody at Circle Daybreak would have anything to do with me. I don't blame them—not after the things my gang did to humans. But it was hard because they wouldn't even talk to me, much less trust me, and they wouldn't believe I wanted to help them. And then you showed up that day after school. And you *did* talk to me—"

"And I did trust you," Hugh said. "And I still do." He looked distant again. "I thought you were the saddest person I'd ever seen, and the most beautiful—and the bravest. I knew you wouldn't betray Circle Daybreak."

And that's why I love you, Jez thought before she could stop herself. It was easier to live with if she didn't put it into words.

Because it was hopeless, of course. You couldn't hang on to an Old Soul. Nobody could—not unless they were one of those tiny fraction of people who were soulmates. Wakened Old Souls were too . . .

old. They knew too much, had seen too much to get attached to any one person.

Much less a person who was tainted with vampire blood.

So all she said was "I know. That's why I work with Circle Daybreak. Because *you* convinced them I wasn't some kind of spy for the Night World. I owe you, Hugh. And—I believe you care about me." Because you care about everybody, she added silently.

Hugh nodded, but he didn't look any happier. "It's about something dangerous. Something I don't want to ask you to do." He dug into his jeans pocket and came up with a thick packet of what looked like folded newspaper articles. He held it out to her.

Jez took it, frowned, then paged through the first few articles. Headlines jumped out at her.

" 'Four-year old dies in coyote attack.' 'Record heatwave in Midwest; hundreds hospitalized.' 'Mother confesses: I killed my babies.' 'Mystery virus erupts in eastern U.S.: Scientists baffled.' "

There were lots more, but she didn't look at them. She looked at Hugh, her eyebrows drawn together. "Thanks for sharing this. Am I supposed to fight the coyote or the virus?"

His lips smiled, but his eyes were bottomless and frighteningly sad. "Nobody can fight what's happening—at least not in the ordinary way. And all that's just the beginning."

"Of *what?*" She loved Hugh, but sometimes she

wanted to strangle him. Old Souls loved being mysterious.

"Have you noticed the weather lately? It's either floods or droughts. Record cold days in winter, record heat in the summer. Record number of hurricanes and tornadoes. Record snowfall and hail. It just gets weirder and weirder every year."

"Well—sure." Jez shrugged. "They talk about it on TV all the time. But it doesn't mean any—"

"And the earth's being disturbed, too. Earthquakes. Volcanoes. Last year four dormant volcanoes erupted and there were dozens of major quakes."

Jez narrowed her eyes. "Okay . . ."

"And there's another weird thing, even though it's not as obvious. You have to kind of dig a little to get to the statistics. There's been an increase in animal attacks all over the world. All kinds of animals." He tapped the pile of newspaper articles. "This coyote attack—a couple of years ago you never heard about coyotes killing kids. Just like you never heard of mountain lions attacking adults. But now it's happening, and it's happening everywhere."

Prickles of unease were going up Jez's arms. It was true, what Hugh was saying. Not that she'd paid much attention to the human news when she was a vampire—but it did seem as if animal attacks were getting more frequent.

"A bunch of elephants stomped their trainers last year," she said slowly.

"Dog attacks are up four hundred percent," Hugh said. "According to the California state police. In

New Mexico there's an epidemic of rabid bats. In Florida they've had *seven* tourists killed by alligators since last January—and believe me, that information was hard to find. Nobody wanted to report it."

"I bet."

"Then there are the insects. We're seeing more and more people get attacked by them. Killer bees. Fire ants. Tiger mosquitoes—and, no, I'm not joking. They're for real, and they carry dengue fever, a really nasty disease."

"Hugh . . ."

"Which brings me to diseases. You have to have noticed that. There are new diseases popping up all over. Ebola. Mad cow disease. That flesh-eating bacteria. Hanta viruses. Lassa. Crimean-Congo hemorrhagic fever. You bleed from your ears and nose and mouth and into the whites of your eyes—"

Jez opened her mouth to say "Hugh" again, but he was racing on, his chest rising and falling quickly, his gray eyes almost feverish.

"And they're resistant to antibiotics the same way that the insects are resistant to pesticides. They're all *mutating*. Changing. Getting stronger and more deadly. And—"

"Hugh." She got it in while he took a breath.

"—there's a hole in the ozone." He looked at her. "What?"

"What does it all *mean*?"

"It means that things are changing. Spiraling out of control. Heading for . . ." He stopped and looked at her. "Jez, it's not those things themselves that are the problem. It's what's behind them."

"And what *is* behind them?"

Hugh said simply, "The Old Powers are rising."

Chills swept over Jez. The Old Powers. The Ancient Magic that had controlled the universe in the old days of the Night World. No one could see or know the Old Powers; they were forces of nature, not people. And they had been sleeping like giant dragons for thousands of years ever since humans had gained control of the world. If they were waking up again now . . .

If magic was coming back again, everything would change.

"It shows in different weird ways," Hugh went on. "Night People are getting more powerful. Lots of them have noticed it. And they say the soulmate principle is back."

The soulmate principle. The idea that for every person there was one destined soulmate, one true love, and that the two souls were bound for eternity. Jez lifted her shoulders and dropped them without meeting Hugh's eyes. "Yeah, I heard. Don't believe it, though."

"I've seen it," Hugh said, and for a moment Jez's heart stopped. Then it started again as he continued, "In other people, I mean. I've seen people our age who found their soulmate, and it's really true; you can see it in their eyes. The Old Powers really *are* rising, Jez . . . for good and for evil. That's what's behind all these other changes."

Jez sat very still. "And so what happens if they keep rising?"

"What happens is . . ." Hugh paused and then looked at her. "It means a time of darkness is coming," he said simply.

"A time—?"

"Of serious darkness. The worst. We're talking the end of the world, here."

Jez could feel gooseflesh on the back of her neck, where her wet hair touched her skin. She might have been tempted to laugh if it were anybody else telling her this. But it was Hugh, and he wasn't joking. She had no desire to laugh.

"But then it's all over," she said. "There's nothing we can do. How can anybody stop the end of the world?"

"Well." He ran a quick hand through his hair, pushing it off his forehead. "That's why I'm here. Because I'm hoping *you* can."

CHAPTER

6

Me?"

Hugh nodded.

"*I'm* supposed to stop the end of the world? *How?*"

"First, I ought to tell you that it's not just me that believes all this about the millennium. It's not even Circle Daybreak that believes it. It's the Night World Council, Jez."

"The joint Council? Witches *and* vampires?"

Hugh nodded again. "They had a big meeting about it this summer. And they dug up some old prophecies about what's going to happen this time."

"Like?"

Hugh looked slightly self-conscious. "Here's one. It used to rhyme in the original, I think, but this is the translation." He took a breath and quoted slowly:

> "In blue fire, the final darkness is banished.
> In blood, the final price is paid."

Great, Jez thought. Whose blood? But Hugh was going on.

> "Four to stand between the light and the shadow,
> Four of blue fire, power in their blood.
> Born in the year of the blind Maiden's vision;
> Four less one and darkness triumphs."

Jez blinked slowly. "What's blue fire?"

"Nobody knows."

" 'Four to stand between the light and the shadow . . .' Meaning to hold off the end of the world?"

"That's what the Council thinks. They think it means that four people have been born, four Wild Powers who're going to be instrumental in whatever's coming, whatever battle or disaster that's going to destroy us. Those four can stop the end of the world—but only if all of them fight together."

" 'Four less one and darkness triumphs,' " Jez said.

"Right. And that's where you come in."

"Sorry, I don't think I'm one of them."

Hugh smiled. "That's not what I meant. The fact is, somebody around here has already reported finding a Wild Power. Circle Daybreak intercepted a message from him to the Council saying that he'll hand the Wild Power over to them if they make it worth his while. Otherwise he'll just sit tight until they're desperate enough to agree to his terms."

Jez had a sinking feeling. She said one word. "Who?"

Hugh's expression was knowing and regretful. "It's one of your old gang, Jez. Morgead Blackthorn."

Jez shut her eyes.

Yeah, that *sounded* like Morgead, trying to shake down the Night World Council. Only *he* was crazy and nervy enough to do that. He was stubborn, too—perfectly capable of letting disaster come if he didn't get his way. But of all the people in the world, why did it have to be him? And how had he found a Wild Power, anyway?

Hugh was speaking again softly. "You can see why we need you. Somebody has to get to him and find out who the Wild Power is—and you're the only one who stands a chance of doing that."

Jez pushed hair off her face and breathed slowly, trying to think.

"I don't need to tell you how dangerous it is," Hugh said, looking into the distance again. "And I don't want to ask you to do it. In fact, if you're smart, you'll tell me to get lost right now."

Jez couldn't tell him to get lost. "What I don't understand is why we can't just let the Council take care of it. They'll want the Wild Powers *bad*, and they have a lot more resources."

Hugh glanced back at her, startled. His gray eyes

were wide with an expression that Jez had never seen before. Then he smiled, and it was an incredibly sad smile.

"That's just what we can't do. You're right, the Council wants the Wild Powers. But not so they can fight the end of the world. Jez . . . they only want them so they can kill them."

That was when Jez realized what his expression was. It was gentle regret for innocence—*her* innocence.

She couldn't believe how stupid she had been.

"Oh, Goddess," she said slowly.

Hugh nodded. "They want it to happen. At least the vampires do. If the human world ends—well, that's their chance, isn't it? For thousands of years the Night People have had to hide, to live in the shadows while the humans spread all over the world. But the Council wants that to change."

The reason Jez had been so slow was that it was hard for her to imagine anybody actually wanting to bring on the Apocalypse. But of course it made sense. "They're willing to risk being destroyed themselves," she whispered.

"They figure that whatever happens, it'll be worse on the humans, since the humans don't know it's coming. Hell, some of the Night People think *they're* what's coming. Hunter Redfern is saying that vampires are going to wipe out and enslave the humans and that after that the Night World is going to reign."

Jez felt a new chill. Hunter Redfern. Her ancestor, who was over five hundred years old but looked about thirty. He was bad, and he practically ran the Council.

"Great," she muttered. "So my family's going to destroy the world."

Hugh gave her a bleak smile. "Hunter says the Old Powers are rising to make vampires stronger so they can take over. And the scary thing is, he's right. Like I said before, the Night People *are* getting stronger, developing more powers. Nobody knows why. But most of the vampires on the Council seem to believe Hunter."

"So we don't have much time," Jez said. "We have to get the Wild Power *before* Morgead makes a deal with the Night World."

"Right. Circle Daybreak is fixing up a safe place to keep the Wild Powers until we get all four. And the Council knows we're doing it—that's probably why that ghoul was following me. They're watching us. I'm just sorry I led it here," he added absently, with a worried look around the room.

"Doesn't matter. He's not telling anybody anything."

"No. Thanks to you. But we'll meet someplace different next time. I can't endanger your family." He looked back at her. "Jez, if the Night World manages to kill even one of the Wild Powers—well, if you believe the prophecy, it's all over."

Jez understood now. She still had questions, but they could wait. One thing was clear in her mind.

"I'll do it. I have to."

Hugh said very quietly, "Are you sure?"

"Well, *somebody* has to. And you were right; I'm the only one who can handle Morgead."

The truth was that she thought nobody could handle Morgead—but she certainly had a better chance than any Circle Daybreaker. Of course, she wouldn't survive the assignment. Even if she managed to steal the Wild Power out from under Morgead's nose, he'd hunt her down and kill her for it.

That was irrelevant.

"He hates me, and I hate him, but at least I *know* him," she said out loud.

There was a silence and she realized that Hugh was looking at her oddly. "You think he hates you?"

"Of course. All we ever did was fight."

Hugh smiled very faintly—an Old Soul look. "I see."

"What's that supposed to mean?"

"It means—I don't think he hates you, Jez. Maybe he has strong emotions for you, but from what I've heard I don't think hate is one of them."

Jez shook her head. "You don't understand. He was always gunning for me. And if he found out I'm half human—well, that would be the end. He hates humans worse than anything. But I think I can fool him for as long as it takes to get the Wild Power."

Hugh nodded, but he didn't look happy. His eyes were bruised and tired. "If you can pull it off, you'll save a lot of lives."

He knows, too, Jez thought. *That I'll die doing this.*

It was some comfort that he cared—and more

comfort that he didn't understand *why* she was doing it. Sure, she wanted to save lives. But there was something else.

The Council had tried to mess with Hugh. They'd sent a stinking *ghoul* after him. They would probably send something different tomorrow—certainly, they'd keep trying to kill him.

And for that, Jez was going to wipe the floor with them. Hugh wasn't any kind of fighter. He couldn't defend himself. He shouldn't be a target.

She realized that Hugh was still looking at her, with pain in his eyes. She smiled to show him that she wasn't afraid of dying.

"It's a family affair," she told him—and that was true, too. "Hunter's my great-great-great-great-great-grandfather. It's only right that I stop him. And if anything happens to me—well, one Redfern less is probably a blessing to the world."

And that was the last part of the truth. She came from a tainted family. No matter what she did, who she saved, or how hard she tried, there would always be vampire blood running in her veins. She was a potential danger to humanity by her very existence.

But Hugh was looking horrified. "Don't you ever say that." He stared at her for another moment and then took her by the shoulders, squeezing. "Jez, you're one of the best people I know. What you did before last year is—"

"Is part of me," Jez said. She was trying not to feel his warm grip through her T-shirt, trying not to show that his little squeeze sent a shock through her entire body. "And nothing can change that. I know what I am."

Hugh shook her slightly. "Jez—"

"And right now, I have to get rid of that ghoul. And you'd better be getting home."

For a moment she thought he was going to shake her again; then he slowly let go of her. "You're officially accepting the assignment?" The way he said it sounded as if he were giving her one last chance not to.

"Yes."

He nodded. He didn't ask *how* she planned on getting back into a gang that she'd abandoned, or getting information from Morgead, who hated her. Jez knew why. He simply trusted that she could do it.

"When you know something, call this number." He dug in a different pocket and handed her a square of paper like a business card. "I'll give you a location where I can meet you—someplace away from here. We shouldn't talk about anything on the phone."

Jez took the card. "Thanks."

"Please be careful, Jez."

"Yes. Can I keep the articles?"

He snorted. "Sure." Then he gave her one of those sad Old-Soul smiles. "You probably don't need them, though. Just look around. Watch the news. You can see it all happening out there."

"We're going to stop it," Jez said. She reconsidered. "We're going to try."

* * *

Jez had a problem the next morning. The problem was Claire.

They were supposed to drive to school together, to ensure that Jez didn't cut school. But Jez had to cut school to go find Morgead. She didn't want to imagine the kind of trouble that was going to get her in with Uncle Jim and Aunt Nanami—but it was crucial to get to Morgead as soon as possible. She couldn't afford to waste time.

At the first major stoplight—and there weren't a lot of them in Clayton—she smacked her forehead with her palm.

"I forgot my chemistry book!" She unfastened her seat belt and slid out of the Audi just as the light turned green. "You go ahead!" she shouted to Claire, slamming the door and leaning in the open window. "I'll catch up to you."

Claire's expression showed her temperature was reaching the boiling point. "Are you crazy? Get in; I'll drive back."

"You'll be late. Go on without me." She made a little fluttery encouraging motion with her fingers.

One of the three cars behind Claire honked.

Claire opened her mouth and shut it again. Her eyes were shooting sparks. "You did this on purpose! I know you're up to something, Jez, and I'm going to find out—"

Honk. Honk.

Jez stepped back and waved goodbye.

And Claire drove off, as Jez had known she would. Claire couldn't stand the peer pressure of cars telling her to get moving.

Jez turned and began to jog for home, in a smooth, steady, ground-eating lope.

When she got there, she wasn't even breathing hard. She opened the garage and picked up a long, slim bundle that had been concealed in a corner. Then she turned to her bike.

Besides Hugh, it was the love of her life. A Harley. An 883 Sportster hugger. Just twenty-seven inches tall and eighty-seven inches long, a lean, light, mean machine. She loved its classic simplicity, its cold clean lines, its spare body. She thought of it as her steel and chrome thoroughbred.

Now she strapped the long bundle diagonally on her back, where it balanced nicely despite its odd size. She put on a dark full-face helmet and swung a leg over the motorcycle. A moment later she was roaring away, heading out of Clayton toward San Francisco.

She enjoyed the ride, even though she knew it might be her last one. Maybe because of that. It was a dazzling end-of-summer day, with a sky of September blue and a pure-white sun. The air that parted for Jez was warm.

How can people ride in cages? she thought, twisting the throttle to shoot past a station wagon. What good are cars? You're completely isolated from your surroundings. You can't hear or smell anything outside; you can't feel wind or Power or a slight change in the temperature. You can't jump out to fight at an instant's notice. You certainly can't stake somebody at high speed while leaning out of a car window.

You could do it from a bike, though. If you were fast enough, you could skewer somebody as you roared by, like a knight with a lance. She and Morgead had fought that way once.

And maybe will again, she thought, and flashed a grim smile into the wind.

The sky remained blue as she continued west, instead of clouding up as she approached the ocean. It was so clear that from Oakland she could see the entire bay and the skyline of San Francisco. The tall buildings looked startlingly close.

She was leaving her own world and entering Morgead's.

It was something she didn't do often. San Francisco was an hour and fifteen minutes away from Clayton—assuming there was no traffic. It might as well have been in another state. Clayton was a tiny rural town, mostly cows, with a few decent houses and one pumpkin farm. As far as Jez knew, the Night World didn't know it existed. It wasn't the kind of place Night People cared about.

Which was why she'd managed to hide there for so long.

But now she was heading straight for the heart of the fire. As she crossed the Bay Bridge and reached the city, she was acutely aware of how vulnerable she was. A year ago Jez had broken the laws of the gang by disappearing. If any gang member saw her, they had the right to kill her.

Idiot. Nobody can recognize you. That's why you wear the full-face helmet. That's why you keep your hair up. That's why you don't custom-paint the bike.

She was still hyper-alert as she cruised the streets heading for one of the city's most unsavory districts.

There. She felt a jolt at the sight of a familiar building. Tan, blocky, and unlovely, it rose to three stories plus an irregular roof. Jez squinted up at the roof without taking off her helmet.

Then she went and stood casually against the rough concrete wall, near the rusty metal intercom. She waited until a couple of girls dressed like artists came up and got buzzed in by one of the tenants. Then she detached herself from the wall and calmly followed them.

She couldn't let Morgead know she was coming.

He'd kill her without waiting to ask questions if he got the jump on her. Her only chance was to jump him first, and then make him listen.

The building was even uglier inside than it was outside, with empty echoing stairwells and faceless industrial-sized hallways. But Jez found her heart beating faster and something like longing twisting in her chest. This place might be hideous, but it was also freedom. Each one of the giant rooms behind the metal doors was rented by somebody who didn't care about carpets and windows, but wanted a big empty space where they could be alone and do exactly what they wanted.

It was mostly starving artists here, people who needed large studios. Some of the doors were painted in gemlike colors and rough textures. Most had industrial-sized locks on them.

I don't miss it, Jez told herself. But every corner brought a shock of memory. Morgead had lived here for years, ever since his mother ran off with some vampire from Europe. And Jez had practically lived here, too, because it had been gang headquarters.

We had some good times. . . .

No. She shook her head slightly to break off the thought and continued on her way, slipping silently through the corridors, going deeper and deeper into the building. At last she got to a place where there was no sound except the humming of the naked fluorescent lights on the ceiling. The walls were closer together here. There was a sense of isolation, of being far from the rest of the world.

And one narrow staircase going up.

Jez paused, listened a moment, then, keeping her eyes on the staircase, removed the long bundle from her back. She unwrapped it carefully, revealing a stick that was a work of art. It was just over four feet long and an inch in diameter. The wood was deep glossy red with irregular black markings that looked a little like tiger stripes or hieroglyphics.

Snakewood. One of the hardest woods in the world, dense and strong, but with just the right amount of resilience for a fighting stick. It made a striking and individual weapon.

There was one other unusual thing about it. Fighting sticks were usually blunt at either end, to allow the person holding it to get a grip. This one had one blunt end and one that tapered to an angled, narrow tip. Like a spear. The point was hard as iron and extremely sharp.

It could punch right through clothing to penetrate a vampire heart.

Jez held the stick in both hands for a moment, looking down at it. Then she straightened, and, holding it in a light grip ready for action, she began up the stairs.

"Ready or not, Morgead, here I come."

CHAPTER

7

She emerged on the rooftop.

There was a sort of roof garden here—anyway, a lot of scraggly plants in large wooden tubs. There was also some dirty patio furniture and other odds and ends. But the main feature was a small structure that sat on the roof the way a house sits on a street.

Morgead's home. The penthouse. It was as stark and unlovely as the rest of the building, but it had a great view and it was completely private. There were no other tall buildings nearby to look down on it.

Jez moved stealthily toward the door. Her feet made no noise on the pitted asphalt of the roof, and she was in a state of almost painfully heightened awareness. In the old days sneaking up on another gang member had been a game. You got to laugh at them if you could startle them, and they got to be furious and humiliated.

Today it wasn't a game.

Jez started toward the warped wooden door—then stopped. Doors were trouble. Morgead would have been an idiot not to have rigged it to alert him to intruders.

Cat-quiet, she headed instead for a narrow metal ladder that led to the roof of the wooden structure. Now she was on the real top of the building. The only thing higher was a metal flagpole without a flag.

She moved noiselessly across the new roof. At the far edge she found herself looking four stories straight down. And directly below her there was a window.

An open window.

Jez smiled tightly.

Then she hooked her toes over the four-inch lip at the edge of the roof and dropped gracefully forward. She grabbed the top of the window in mid-dive and hung suspended, defying gravity like a bat attached upside down. She looked inside.

And there he was. Lying on a futon, asleep. He was sprawled on his back, fully clothed in jeans, high boots, and a leather jacket. He looked good.

Just like the old days, Jez thought. When the gang would stay out all night riding their bikes and hunting or fighting or partying, and then come home in the morning to scramble into clothes for school. Except Morgead, who would smirk at them and then collapse. He didn't have parents or relatives to keep him from skipping.

I'm surprised he's not wearing his helmet, too, she thought, pulling herself back up to the roof. She picked up the fighting stick, maneuvered it into the window, then let herself down again, this time hanging by her hands. She slid in without making a noise.

Then she went to stand over him.

He hadn't changed. He looked exactly as she remembered, except younger and more vulnerable because he was asleep. His face was pale, making his dark hair seem even darker. His lashes were black crescents on his cheeks.

Evil and dangerous, Jez reminded herself. It annoyed her that she *had* to remind herself of what Morgead was. For some reason her mind was throwing pictures at her, scenes from her childhood while she was living here in San Francisco with her Uncle Bracken.

A five-year-old Jez, with shorter red hair that looked as if it had never been combed, walking with a little grimy-faced Morgead, hand in hand. An eight-year-old Jez with two skinned knees, scowling as a businesslike Morgead pulled wood splinters out of her legs with rusty tweezers. A seven-year-old Morgead with his face lit up in astonishment as Jez persuaded him to try the human thing called ice cream. . . .

Stop it, Jez told her brain flatly. You might as well give up, because it's no good. We were friends then—well, some of the time—but we're enemies now. He's changed. I've changed. He'd kill me in a second now if it would suit his purpose. And I'm going to do what has to be done.

She backed up and poked him lightly with the stick. "Morgead."

His eyes flew open and he sat up. He was awake instantly, like any vampire, and he focused on her without a trace of confusion. Jez had changed her grip on the stick and was standing ready in case he went straight into an attack.

But instead, a strange expression crossed his face. It went from startled recognition into something Jez didn't understand. For a moment he was simply staring at her, eyes big, chest heaving, looking as if he were caught in between pain and happiness.

Then he said quietly, "Jez."

"Hi, Morgead."

"You came back."

Jez shifted the stick again. "Apparently."

He got up in one motion. "Where the hell have you *been*?"

Now he just looked furious, Jez noted. Which was easier to deal with, because that was how she remembered him.

"I can't tell you," she said, which was perfectly true, and would also annoy the life out of him.

It did. He shook his head to get dark hair out of his eyes—it was always disheveled in the morning, Jez remembered—and glared at her. He was standing easily: not in any attack posture, but with the relaxed readiness that meant he could go flying in any direction at any moment. Jez kept half her mind on watching his leg muscles.

"You can't *tell* me? You disappear one day without any kind of warning, without even leaving a *note* . . . you leave the gang and me and just completely vanish and nobody knows where to find you, not even your uncle . . . and now you reappear again and *you can't tell me where you were?*" He was working himself into one of his Extremely Excited States, Jez realized. She was surprised; she'd expected him to stay cooler and attack hard.

"What did you think you were doing, just cutting out on everybody? Did it ever occur to you that people would be *worried* about you? That people would think you were *dead?*"

It didn't occur to me that anyone would *care*, Jez thought, startled. Especially not you. But she couldn't say that. "Look, I didn't mean to hurt anybody. And I can't talk about why I went. But I'm back now—"

"You can't just come back!"

Jez was losing her calm. Nothing was going the way she'd expected; the things she'd scripted out to say weren't getting said. "I know I can't just come back—"

"Because it doesn't work that way!" Morgead was pacing now, tossing hair out of his eyes again as he turned to glare at her. "Blood in, blood out. Since you're apparently not dead, you abandoned us. You're not allowed to do that! And you certainly can't expect to just walk back in and become my second again—"

"I *don't!*" Jez yelled. She had to shut him up. "I have no intention of becoming your second-in-command!" she said when he finally paused. "I came to challenge you as leader."

Morgead's jaw dropped.

Jez let her breath out. That wasn't exactly how she'd planned to say it. But now, seeing his shock, she felt more in control. She leaned casually against the wall, smiled at him, and said smoothly, "I was leader when I left, remember."

"You . . . have got to be . . . joking." Morgead stared at her. "You expect to waltz back in here as *leader?*"

"If I can beat you. I think I can. I did it once."

He stared for another minute, seeming beyond words. Then he threw back his head and laughed.

It was a scary sound.

When he looked at her again, his eyes were bright and hard. "Yeah, you did. I've gotten better since then."

Jez said three words. "So have I."

And with that, everything changed. Morgead shifted position—only slightly, but he was now in a fighting stance. Jez felt adrenaline flow through her own body. The challenge had been issued and accepted; there was nothing more to say. They were now facing each other ready to fight.

And this she could deal with. She was much better at fighting than at playing with words. She knew Morgead in this mood; his pride and his skill had been questioned and he was now absolutely determined to win. This was very familiar.

Without taking his eyes from her, he reached out and picked a fighting stick from the rack behind him.

Japanese oak, Jez noted. Heavy, well-seasoned, resilient. Good choice.

The fire-hardened end was very pointy.

He wouldn't try to use that first, though. First, he would go for disarming her. The simplest way to do this was to break the wrist of her dominant hand. After that he'd go for critical points and nerve centers. He didn't play around at this.

A minute change in Morgead's posture alerted her, and then they were both moving.

He swung his stick up and down in a perfect arc, aiming for her right wrist. Jez blocked easily with her own stick and felt the shock as wood clashed with wood. She instantly changed her grip and tried for a trap, but he whipped his stick out of the way and was facing her again as if he'd never moved in the first place.

He smiled at her.

He's right. He's gotten better. A small chill went through Jez, and for the first time she worried about her ability to beat him.

Because I have to do it without *killing* him, she thought. She wasn't at all sure he had the same concern about not killing her.

"You're so predictable, Morgead," she told him. "I could fight you in my sleep." She feinted toward his wrist and then tried to sweep his legs out from underneath him.

He blocked and tried for a trap. "Oh, yeah? And

you hit like a four-year-old. You couldn't take me down if I stood here and let you."

They circled each other warily.

The snakewood stick was warm in Jez's hands. It was funny, some distant part of her mind thought irrelevantly, how the most humble and lowly of human weapons was the most dangerous to vampires.

But it was also the most versatile weapon in the world. With a stick, unlike a knife or gun or sword, you could fine-tune the degree of pain and injury you caused. You could disarm and control attackers, and—if the circumstances required it—you could inflict pain without permanently injuring them.

Of course if they were vampires, you could also *kill* them, which you couldn't do with a knife or gun. Only wood could stop the vampire heart permanently, which was why the fighting stick was the weapon of choice for vampires who wanted to hurt each other . . . and for vampire hunters.

Jez grinned at Morgead, knowing it was not a particularly nice smile.

Her feet whispered across the worn oak boards of the floor. She and Morgead had practiced here countless times, measuring themselves against each other, training themselves to be the best. And it had worked. They were both masters of this most deadly weapon.

But no fight had ever mattered as much as this one.

"Next you're going to try for a head strike," she

informed Morgead coolly. "Because you always do."

"You think you know everything. But you don't know me anymore. I've changed," he told her, just as calmly—and went for a head strike.

"Psyche," he said as she blocked it and wood clashed with a sharp *whack*.

"Wrong." Jez twisted her stick sharply, got leverage on his, and whipped it down, holding it against his upper thighs. "Trap." She grinned into his face.

And was startled for a moment. She hadn't been this close to him in a long time. His eyes—they were *so* green, gem-colored, and full of strange light.

For just an instant neither of them moved; their weapons down, their gazes connected. Their faces were so close their breath mingled.

Then Morgead slipped out of the trap. "Don't try *that* stuff," he said nastily.

"What stuff?" The moment her stick was free of his, she snapped it up again, reversing her grip and thrusting toward his eyes.

"You know what stuff!" He deflected her thrust with unnecessary force. "That 'I'm Jez and I'm so wild and beautiful' stuff. That 'Why don't you just drop your stick and let me hit you because it'll be fun' stuff."

"Morgead . . . what are you . . . talking about?" In between the words she attacked, a strike to his throat and then one to his temple. He blocked and evaded—which was just what she wanted. Evasion. Retreat. She was crowding him into a corner.

"That's the only way you won before. Trying to play on people's feelings for you. Well, it won't work anymore!" He countered viciously, but it didn't matter. Jez blocked with a whirlwind of strikes of her own, pressing him, and then he had no choice but to retreat until his back was against the corner.

She had him.

She had no idea what he meant about playing on people's feelings, and she didn't have time to think about it. Morgead was dangerous as a wounded tiger when he was cornered. His eyes were glowing emerald green with sheer fury, and there was a hardness to his features that hadn't been there last year.

He does hate me, Jez thought. Hugh was wrong. He's hurt and angry and he absolutely *hates* me.

The textbook answer was to use that emotion against him, to provoke him and get him so mad that he gave her an opening. Some instinct deep inside Jez was worried about that, but she didn't listen.

"Hey, all's fair, right?" she told him softly. "And what do you mean, it won't work? I've got you, haven't I?" She flashed out a couple of quick attacks, more to keep him occupied than anything else. "You're caught, and you're going to have to let down your guard sometime."

The green eyes that had been luminous with fury suddenly went cold. The color of glacier ice. "Unless I do something unexpected," he said.

"Nothing you do is unexpected," she said sweetly.

But her mind was telling her that provoking him had been a mistake. She had hit some nerve, and he was stronger than he'd been a year ago. He didn't lose his temper under pressure the way he'd used to. He just got more determined.

Those green eyes unnerved her.

Move in hard, she thought. All out. Go for a pressure point. Numb his arm—

But before she could do anything, a wave of Power hit her.

It sent her reeling.

She'd never felt anything exactly like it. It came from Morgead, a shockwave of telepathic energy that struck her like a physical thing. It knocked her back two steps and made her struggle for balance. It left the air crackling with electricity and a faint smell of ozone.

Jez's mind spun.

How had he *done* that?

"It's not hard," Morgead said in a calm, cold voice that went with his eyes. He was out of the corner by now, of course. For a moment Jez thought he was reading her thoughts, but then she realized her question must be written all over her face. "It's something I discovered after you left," he went on. "All it takes is practice."

If you're telepathic, Jez thought. Which I'm not anymore.

The Night People are getting stronger, developing more powers, she thought. Well, Hugh had been right on that one.

And she was in trouble now.

Whack! That was Morgead going for a side sweep. He'd noticed her lack of balance. Jez countered automatically, but her head wasn't clear and her body was ringing with pain. He'd shaken her, distracted her.

"As you said, all's fair," Morgead said, with a small, cold smile on his lips. "You have your weapons. I have mine."

And then he threw another of those shockwaves at her. Jez was better braced for it now, but it still rocked her on her feet, took her attention off her weapon—

Just long enough for her to screw up and let him in.

He drove upward to catch her stick from below. Then he twisted, sweeping her stick in a circle, forcing her off balance again, trying to topple her backward. As Jez fought to recover, he struck to her elbow. Hard.

Wham!

It was a different sound from the crisp *whack* when wood hit wood. This was softer, duller, the sound of wood hitting flesh and bone.

Jez heard her own involuntary gasp of pain.

Fire shot up her arm, into her shoulder, and for a moment she lost her grip on the stick with her right hand. She forced her fingers to close on it again, but they were numb. She couldn't feel what she was holding.

She couldn't block properly with one arm useless.

And Morgead was advancing, that deadly cold

light in his eyes. Absolutely merciless. His movements were relaxed and easy; he knew exactly what he was doing now.

Two more whacks and he got through her guard again. The oak stick slammed into her ribs and she felt another wave of sickening pain. Gray dots danced in front of her eyes.

Fractured? Jez wondered briefly. She hoped not. Vampires could break each other's ribs in fun and know that everything would heal in a day or two. But Jez wouldn't recover like that. Morgead might kill her without even meaning to.

She couldn't let him keep striking her—but she couldn't retreat, either. If he got her into a corner, she'd be lost.

Whack-wham. He got her on the knee. Pain sparked up and down her leg, lighting every nerve. She had no choice but to back up. He was crowding her relentlessly, forcing her to the wall.

Morgead flashed a smile at her. Not the cold smile. This one was brilliant, and very familiar to Jez. It made him look devastatingly handsome, and it meant that he was in absolute command of the situation.

"You can give up anytime, now," he said. "Because I'm going to win and we both know it."

CHAPTER

8

I can't lose this fight.

Suddenly that was the only thought in Jez's mind. She couldn't afford to be hurt or scared—or stupid. There was too much riding on it.

And since Morgead had the advantages of telepathy and strength on her at the moment, she was going to have to come up with some clever way to beat him.

It only took a moment to come up with a plan. And then Jez was carrying it out, every ounce of her concentration focused on tricking him.

She stopped backing up and took a step sideways, deliberately putting herself in a position where she could make only a clumsy block. Then she gave him an opening, holding her stick awkwardly, its tip toward him but drooping too far down.

You see—it's my elbow, she thought to him, knowing he couldn't hear her, but willing him to take the bait. My elbow hurts too much; I'm distracted; the stick is no longer an extension of me. My right side is unprotected.

She was as good at it as any mother bird who pretends to have a broken wing to lure a predator away from her nest. And she could see the flash of triumph in Morgead's eyes.

That's it; don't waste time injuring me anymore . . . come in for the kill.

He was doing it. He'd stopped trying to get her into a corner. With his handsome face intent, his eyes narrowed in concentration, he was maneuvering for a single decisive strike; a takedown to end the combat.

But as he raised his fighting stick to make it, Jez pulled her own stick back as if she were afraid to block, afraid of the jarring contact. This was the moment. If he caught on now, if he realized why she was positioning her stick this way, he'd never make the move she wanted him to. He'd go back to disarming her.

I'm too hurt to block properly; my arm's too weak to raise, she thought, letting her shoulders droop and her body sway tiredly. It wasn't hard to pretend. The pain in various parts of her body was real enough, and if she let herself *feel* it, it was very nearly disabling.

Morgead fell for it.

He made the strike she wanted; straight down. At that instant Jez slid her leading foot back, shifting just out of range. His stick whistled by her nose—missing. And then, before he could raise it again, while he was unguarded, Jez lunged. She put all the power of her body behind it, all her strength, slipping in between Morgead's arms and driving the stick to his midsection.

The air in his lungs exploded out in a harsh gasp and he doubled over.

Jez didn't hesitate. She had to finish him instantly, because in a second he would be fully recovered. By the time he was completely bent over she was already whipping her stick out and around to strike him behind the knee. Again, she put her whole weight behind the blow, following through to scoop him onto his back.

Morgead landed with a thud. Before he could move, Jez snap-kicked hard, catching his wrist and knocking his stick away. It clattered across the floor, oak on oak.

Then she held the pointed end of her own stick to his throat.

"Yield or die," she said breathlessly, and smiled.

Morgead glared up at her.

He was even more breathless than she was, but there was nothing like surrender in those green eyes. He was *mad*.

"You tricked me!"

"All's fair."

He just looked at her balefully from under the disordered hair that fell across his forehead. He was sprawled flat, long legs stretched out, arms flung to either side, with the tip of the snakewood fighting stick resting snugly in the pale hollow of his throat. He was completely at her mercy—or at least that was how it seemed.

Jez knew him better.

She knew that he never gave up, and that when he wasn't too mad to think, he was as smart as she was. And as sneaky. Right now the helpless act was about as sincere as her wounded bird routine.

So she was ready when he threw another blast of Power at her. She saw his pupils dilate like a cat's about to pounce, and she braced herself, shifting the stick minutely to push into his collarbone as she leaned forward.

The energy smashed into her. She could almost see it now, with the sixth sense that was part of her vampire heritage. It was like the downrush of a nuclear cloud, the part that went flowing along the ground, destroying everything in its path, spreading in a circle from the point of impact. It seemed to be faintly green, the color of Morgead's eyes. And it packed quite a punch.

Jez gritted her teeth and hung on to the fighting stick, keeping it in place, letting the Power wash through her. It blew her hair back to stream in a hot wind and it seemed to last forever.

But finally it was over, and she was tingling with pain, with a metallic feeling in her teeth. And Morgead was still trapped.

He hissed at her, an amazingly reptilian sound.

"Got anything else?" Jez said, grinning down at him with narrowed eyes. Every bruise on her body hurt afresh in the aftermath of the blast—but she wasn't going to let him see that. "No? I didn't think so."

Morgead's upper lip lifted. "Drop dead, Jezebel."

Nobody was allowed to use her full name. "You first, Morgy," she suggested, and leaned harder on the stick.

The green eyes were beautifully luminous now, with sheer anger and hatred. "So kill me," he said nastily.

"Morgead—"

"It's the only way you're going to win. Otherwise I'm just going to lie here and wait to recharge. And when I've got enough Power I'll hit you again."

"You never know when it's over, do you?"

"It's never over."

Jez bit down on a rush of fury and exasperation. "I didn't want to have to do this," she snarled, "but I will."

She didn't kill him. Instead, she hurt him.

She grabbed his wrist and locked it, with her hand holding his and her stick on top of his wrist. She could use leverage here to cause severe pain— or to break the bone.

"Give up, Morgead."

"Bite me."

"I'm going to break your wrist."

"Fine. I hope you enjoy it." He kept glaring.

Like a little kid threatening to play on the freeway, Jez thought, and suddenly, inexplicably she was almost overcome by laughter. She choked it back.

She didn't *want* to break his wrist. But she knew

she had to. And she had to do it soon, before he regenerated enough Power to hit her again. She couldn't take another of those blasts.

"Morgead, give!" She put enough pressure on his wrist that it really hurt.

He gave her the evil eye through dark lashes.

"You're so stubborn!" Jez put on more pressure.

She could tell it was hurting him. It was hurting *her* to keep the steady pressure up. Shooting stars of pain were zinging in her elbow.

Jez's heart was beating hard and her muscles were beginning to tremble with fatigue. This was much more difficult for both of them than a clean break would have been. And he was a vampire— his wrist would heal in a few days. She wouldn't be injuring him permanently.

I *have* to do it, she told herself. She tensed her muscles—

And Morgead took a little quick breath, an indrawn hiss of pain. For just an instant his green eyes lost their gemlike clarity, unfocusing a bit as he winced.

Jez let go of his wrist and collapsed to sit beside him, breathing hard.

You are *so* stupid, her mind told her. She shook her hair out and shut her eyes, trying to deal with the fury.

Beside her, Morgead sat up. "What are you doing?"

"I don't know!" Jez snarled without opening her eyes. Being weak and idiotic, she answered herself. She didn't even know *why* she couldn't go through with it. She killed vampires—and less obnoxious ones than Morgead—all the time.

"I didn't yield," Morgead said. His voice was flat and dangerous. "So it's not over."

"Fine, blast me."

"I'm going to."

"So do it."

"What, you like it so much?"

Jez snapped. She grabbed her stick off the ground and turned to look at him for the first time since she'd sat down. "Yeah, I love it, Morgead! I'm crazy about pain! So do it, and then I'm going to hit you over your thick head so hard you won't wake up until next week!" She might have said more, but the look in his eyes stopped her.

He was staring at her intently, not simply belligerently as she'd imagined. His green eyes were narrow and searching.

"You're just crazy period," he said, sitting back, his gaze still probing. In a different tone he said softly, "So why didn't you do it?"

Jez lifted her shoulders and dropped them. There was a pit of anger and misery in her stomach. "I suppose because then I'd have to break every bone in your body, you jerk. You'd never give up, not with that new power you've got."

"I could teach it to you. The others aren't strong enough to learn it, but you are."

That forced a short laugh out of Jez. "Yeah, right." She shut her eyes briefly, wondering what Morgead would say if she were to tell him *why* she could never learn it.

He'd squash me like a bug, she thought, and laughed again.

"You laugh weird, Jez."

"I have a twisted sense of humor." She looked at him, blinking wetness out of her lashes. Where had that come from? There must be something in her eye. "So. Want to start this fight again?"

He was staring at her hand gripping the snakewood stick. Jez tried to keep that hand steady, but she could feel the fine tremors in the muscles. She took a deep breath and clenched her teeth, making her gaze challenging.

I can fight again. I can do it because I have to, and this time I won't let any stupid sympathy get in the way of beating him. I *have* to win. Everything depends on it.

Morgead looked back at her face. "No," he said abruptly. "We don't have to do it again. I yield."

Jez blinked in shock. It was the last thing she'd expected. Morgead's expression was cold and unreadable.

Jez got mad.

"Why?" she blazed at him. "Because I'm tired? Because you don't think I can take you?" She whipped the stick up, ready to split his stupid skull.

"Because you're crazy!" Morgead yelled. "And because—" He stopped dead, looked furious. Then he said curtly, "Because you won fair the first time."

Jez stared at him.

Slowly she lowered the stick.

Morgead's expression was still distinctly unfriendly. But he'd just made an almost unbelievable admission.

"You just don't want me to whop you anymore," she said.

He gave her a sideways look that would kill pigeons in midair.

Jez let out her breath. Her heart was just beginning to settle down and relief was spreading through her.

I did it. I really did it. I'm not going to die today.

"So it's over," she said. "I'm back in."

"You're leader," Morgead said sourly. "Enjoy it, because I'm going to be right behind you every step, just waiting for my chance."

"I wouldn't expect anything else," Jez said. Then she blinked. "What are you doing?"

"What do you think?" His face set, his eyes on the far wall, Morgead was tugging his shirt away from his neck, and leaning his head back.

"I have no idea—" Then Jez realized. She went cold to the tips of her fingers.

I didn't think. I should have remembered, but I didn't, and I didn't plan for this. . . .

"Blood in, blood out," Morgead said shortly.

Why didn't I remember? Panic was stirring inside Jez. She couldn't see any way to get out of it.

For human gangs "blood in, blood out" meant you got beat up when you were jumped in, and you didn't leave until you were dead. But for vampire gangs . . .

I can't bite him.

The most frightening thing was that something

inside her wanted to do it. Her entire skin was tingling, and it suddenly seemed as if it was only yesterday that she'd had her last blood meal. She could remember exactly how it felt, sinking her teeth into smooth skin, piercing it easily, feeling the warm flow start.

And Morgead's blood would be dark and sweet and powerful. Vampire blood wasn't life-sustaining like human blood, but it was rich with the hidden promise of the Night World. And Morgead was one of the strongest vampires she'd ever met. His blood would be full of the mastery of that new attack, full of raw, vital young energy.

But I don't drink blood. I'm not a vampire! Not anymore.

Jez was trembling in shock. In the entire year since she'd stopped drinking blood, she'd never been so tempted. She had no idea why it had come on like this now, but it was almost out of her control. She pressed her tongue against one sharpening canine, trying to restrain it, trying to get some relief from the stress. Her upper and lower jaws were aching fiercely.

I can't. It's unthinkable. If I do it once, I'll never be able to stop. I'll become—what I was back then.

I'll be lost.

I can't—but I have to. I need to get back in the gang.

Morgead was staring at her. "Now what's wrong with you?"

"I . . ." Jez was dizzy with fear and longing and

the sense of danger. She couldn't see any way out. . . .

And then she saw it.

"Here," she said, unbuttoning the collar of her shirt. "You bite me."

"*What?*"

"It satisfies the requirement. Blood has to be spilled. And it's the leader who does it."

"*You're* the leader, idiot."

"Not until I'm back in the gang. And I'm not back in the gang until blood is spilled."

He was staring at her, his eyes hard and demanding and not amused at all. "Jez . . . that's ridiculous. *Why?*"

He was too smart. She didn't dare let him keep thinking about it. "Because I think it's the proper procedure. And because—I overfed last night. I don't want anymore." She stared straight into his eyes, not allowing a muscle to quiver. Trying to force her version of the truth into his brain.

Morgead blinked and looked away.

Jez allowed herself to relax minutely. She had one advantage over Morgead; there was no way he could even imagine her real motives. She just hoped he wouldn't discern the human flavor to her blood.

"If you won't tell me, I give up." He shrugged. "So, fine. If that's the way you want it . . ."

"It is."

"Whatever." He turned back to her and reached for her shoulders.

A new shock rocked Jez. Morgead never hesitated

once he made up his mind, but this was a little unnerving. His grip was a bit too firm and authoritative; Jez felt out of control.

And how am I going to shield myself? she thought wildly, clamping down on a new wave of fear. He's already a powerful telepath and sharing blood increases rapport. How am I supposed to block *that*—?

Everything was happening too fast; she didn't have time to plan or think. All she could do was try not to panic as Morgead drew her close.

Jerk . . . he's had too much experience at this, part of her thought furiously. At subduing any kind of prey. At gentling scared girls—human girls.

He was holding her lightly and precisely; he was tilting her chin back. Jez shut her eyes and tried to blank her mind.

And now she could feel the warmth of his face near her skin; she could feel his breath on her throat. She knew his canine teeth were extending, lengthening, thinning to needle points. She tried to control her breathing.

She felt a swathe of warmth as he licked her throat once, and then a pain that made her own teeth ache. His teeth had pierced her skin, sharp as obsidian.

Then the release of blood flowing. Her life, spilling out. The instinctive twinge of fear Jez felt had nothing to do with him invading her mind.

No vampire liked to make this kind of submission. Letting someone drink your blood meant you were weaker, it meant you were willingly making yourself prey. Everything inside Jez protested at just relaxing and letting Morgead do this.

And maybe that was the answer, she thought suddenly. A wall of turmoil to cover her thoughts. Pretend to be too agitated to let him make contact. . . .

But his lips were surprisingly soft on her throat, and the pain was gone, and he was holding her more like a lover than like a predator. She could feel his mind all around her, strong, demanding.

He wasn't trying to hurt her. He was trying to make it not-terrible for her.

But I want it to be terrible. I don't want to feel like this. . . .

It didn't matter. She felt as if she were being pulled by a swift current, dragged and tumbled into some place she had never been before. Sparkling lights danced behind her closed eyelids. Electricity crackled through her body.

And then she felt his mouth moving gently on her throat, and the world fell away. . . .

CHAPTER

No. This can't be happening.

Jez had never felt anything like this before, but she knew instinctively that it was dangerous. She was being pulled into Morgead's *mind*. She could feel it surrounding her, enfolding her, a touch that was light but almost irresistible, that was trying to draw out the most secret part of herself.

And the most frightening thing was that Morgead wasn't doing it.

It was something outside both of them, something that was trying to mix them together like two pools of water being stirred. Jez could feel that Morgead was as startled and astonished as she was. The only difference was that he didn't seem to be resisting the force. He didn't seem terrified and unhappy about it, as Jez was. He seemed . . . exhilarated and wondering, like somebody skydiving for the first time.

That's because he's *crazy,* Jez thought dizzily. He loves danger and he enjoys courting death—

I enjoy you, a voice said in her mind.

Morgead's voice. Soft as a whisper, a feather-touch that shook Jez to her soul.

It had been so long since she'd heard that voice.

And he had heard *her.* Sharing blood made even humans telepathic. Jez hadn't been able to talk mentally since—

She managed to cut the thought off as panic surged through her. While one part of her mind gabbled desperately, "He's here, he's here, he's *inside,* what are we going to do now?" another part threw up a smokescreen, flooding her thoughts with visions of mist and clouds.

There was something like a swift gasp from Morgead.

Jez, don't. Don't hide from me—

You're not allowed here, she snapped back, this time directing the thought straight at him. *Go away!*

I can't. For just a moment his mental voice sounded confused and scared. She hadn't realized Morgead could *be* confused and scared. *I'm not doing this. It's just—happening.*

But it shouldn't be happening, Jez thought, and she didn't know whether she was talking to him or just to herself. She was beginning to shake. She couldn't resist the pull that was trying to bring her soul to the surface and intermingle it with Morgead's—she *couldn't*. It was stronger than anything she'd ever experienced. But she knew that if she gave in, she was dead.

Don't be afraid. Don't, Morgead said in a voice she had never heard from him before. A voice of desperate gentleness. His mind was trying to wrap around hers protectively, like dark wings shielding her, touching her softly.

Jez felt her insides turn to water.

No. *No . . .*

Yes, Morgead's voice whispered.

She had to stop this—now. She had to break the contact. But although Jez could still feel her physical body, she seemed powerless to control it. She could sense Morgead's arms supporting her and his lips on her throat and she knew that he was still drinking. But she couldn't so much as move a finger to push him away. The muscles that she'd trained so ruthlessly to obey her under any circumstances were betraying her now.

She had to try another way.

This shouldn't be happening, she told Morgead, putting all the energy of her terror behind the thought.

I know. But that's because you're fighting it. We should be somewhere else by now.

Jez was exasperated. *Where else?*

I don't know, he said, and she could feel a tinge of sadness in his thought. *Some place—deeper. Where we'd really be together. But you won't open your mind. . . .*

Morgead, what are you talking about? What do you think is going on?

He seemed genuinely surprised. *Don't you know? It's the soulmate principle.*

Jez felt the floor drop away beneath her.

No. That's not possible. That can't *be*. She wasn't talking to Morgead anymore; she was desperately trying to convince herself. I'm not soulmates with Morgead. I can't be. We hate each other . . . he hates me . . . all we ever do is fight. . . .

He's impossible and dangerous and hotheaded and stubborn . . . he's crazy . . . he's angry and hostile . . . he's frustrating and infuriating and he loves to make me miserable . . .

And I don't even believe in soulmates. And even if I did, I wouldn't believe it could happen like this, just bang, out of the blue, like getting hit by a train when you're not looking, without any warning or even any attraction to the person beforehand. . . .

But the very hysteria of her own thoughts was a bad sign. Anything that could tear away her self-control like this was powerful almost beyond imagination. And she could still feel it pulling at her, trying to strip off the layers of cloud she was hiding behind. It wanted Morgead to *see* her as she truly was.

And it was trying to show her Morgead. Flashes of his life, of himself. Glimpses that hit her and seemed to cut cleanly through her, leaving her gasping with their intensity.

A little boy with a mop of tousled dark hair and eyes like emerald, watching his mother walk out the door with some man—again. Going to play alone in the darkness, amusing himself. And then meeting a little redheaded girl, a girl with silvery-blue eyes and a flashing smile. And not being alone anymore. And walking on fences with her in the cool night air, chasing small animals, falling and giggling. . . .

A slightly older boy with longer hair that fell around his face, uncared-for. Watching his mother walk out one last time, never to come back. Hunting for food, sleeping in an empty house that got messier and messier. Learning to care for himself. Training himself. Getting harder, in mind and body, seeing a sullen expression when he looked in the mirror . . .

A boy even older watching humans, who were weak and silly and short-lived, but who had all the things he didn't have. Family, security, food every night. Watching the Night People, the elders, who felt no responsibility to help an abandoned vampire child. . . .

I never knew, Jez thought. She still felt dizzy, as if she couldn't get enough air. The images were dazzling in their clarity and they tore at her heart.

A boy who started a gang to create a family, and who went first to the little girl with red hair. The two of them grinning wickedly, running wild in the streets, finding others. Collecting kids the adults couldn't control or wouldn't miss. Walking around the worst parts of town, unafraid—because they had one another now.

The images were coming faster, and Jez could hardly keep up with them.

Dashing through the metal scrap yard . . . with Jez . . . Hiding under a fish-smelling wharf . . . from Jez . . . His first big kill, a stag in the hills of San Rafael . . . and Jez there to share the hot blood that warmed and intoxicated and brought life all at once. Fear and happiness and anger and arguments, hurt and sadness and exasperation—but always with Jez interwoven into the fabric. She was always there in his memories, fire-colored hair streaming behind her, heavy-lashed eyes snapping with challenge and excitement. She was everything bright and eager and brave and honest. She was haloed with flame.

I didn't know . . . how could I know? How could I realize I meant so much to him . . . ?

And who would have thought it would mean so much to her when she found out? She was stunned, overcome—but something inside her was singing, too.

She was *happy* about it. She could feel something bubbling up that she hadn't even realized was there; a wild and heady delight that seemed to shoot out to the palms of her hands and the soles of her feet.

Morgead, she whispered with her mind.

She could sense him, but for once he didn't answer. She felt his sudden fear, his own desire to run and hide. He hadn't meant to show her these things. They were being forced out of him by the same power that was dragging at Jez.

I'm sorry. I didn't mean to look, she thought to him. *I'll go away. . . .*

No. Suddenly he wasn't hiding anymore. *No, I don't want you to go. I want you to stay.*

Jez felt herself flow toward him, helplessly. The truth was that she didn't know if she could turn away even if he'd wanted her to. She could feel his mind touching hers—she could taste the very essence of his soul. And it made her tremble.

This was like nothing she'd ever felt before. It was so strange . . . but so wonderful. A pleasure that she couldn't have dreamed of. To be this close, and to be getting closer, like fire and bright darkness merging . . . To feel her mind opening to him . . .

And then the distant echo of fear, like an animal screaming a warning.

Are you insane? This is *Morgead.* Let him see your soul . . . pry open your innermost secrets . . . and you won't live long enough to regret it. He'll tear your throat out the instant he finds out . . .

Jez flinched wildly from the voice. She didn't want to resist the pull to Morgead any longer. But fear was shivering through her, poisoning the warmth and closeness, freezing the edges of her mind. And she knew that the voice was the only rationality left in her.

Do you want to die? it asked her point-blank.

Jez, Morgead was saying quietly. *What's wrong? Why won't you let it happen?*

Not just you dying, the voice said. All those others. Claire and Aunt Nan and Uncle Jim and Ricky. Hugh . . .

Something white-hot flickered through her. Hugh. Whom she loved. Who couldn't fight for himself. She hadn't even *thought* of him since she'd entered Morgead's mind—and that terrified her.

How could she have forgotten him? For the last year Hugh had represented everything good to her. He'd awakened feelings in her that she'd never had before. And he was the one person she would never betray.

Jez, Morgead said.

Jez did the only thing she could think of. She threw an image at him, a picture to stir his memories. A picture of her walking out, leaving the gang, leaving him.

It wasn't a real picture, of course. It was a symbol.

It was bait.

And she felt it hit Morgead's mind and clash there, and strike memories that flew like sparks.

The first meeting of the gang with her not there. Questions. Puzzlement. All of them searching for her, trying to find a hint of her unique Power signature on the streets. At first laughing as they called for her, making it a game, then the laughter turning into annoyance as she stayed missing. Then annoyance turning into worry.

Her uncle Bracken's house. The gang crowded on the doorstep with Morgead in front. Uncle Bracken looking lost and sad. "I don't know where she is. She just—disappeared." And worry turning into gut-wrenching fear. Fear and anger and sorrow and betrayal.

If she wasn't dead, then she'd abandoned him. Just like everyone else. Just like his mother.

And that grief and fury building, both perfectly balanced because Morgead didn't know which was the truth. But always with the knowledge, either way, that the world was cold because she was gone.

And then . . . her appearing in his room today. Obviously alive. Insultingly healthy. And unforgivably casual as she told him he would never know why she'd left.

Jez felt Morgead's outrage swelling up, a dark wave inside him, a coldness that felt no mercy for anyone and only wanted to hurt and kill. It was filling him, sweeping everything else away. Just being in contact with it started her heart pounding and shortened her breath. Its raw violence was terrifying.

You left me! he snarled at her, three syllables with a world of bitterness behind them.

I had to. And I'll never tell you why. Jez could feel her own eyes stinging; she supposed he could sense how it hurt her to say that. But it was the only thing that would work. The pull between them was weakening, being smashed away by his anger.

You're a traitor, he said. And the image behind it was that of everyone who'd ever betrayed a friend or a lover or a cause for the most selfish of reasons. Every betrayer from the history of the human world or the Night World. That was what Morgead thought of her.

I don't care what you think, she said.

You never cared, he shot back. *I know that now. I don't know why I ever thought differently.*

The force that had been trying to drag them together had thinned to a silver thread of connection. And that was good—it was *necessary,* Jez told herself. She made an effort and felt herself slide away from Morgead's mind, and then further, and then further.

You'd better not forget it again, she said. It was easier to be nasty when she couldn't feel his reactions. *It might be bad for your health.*

Don't worry, he told her briefly. *I can take care of myself. And you'd better believe I'll never forget.*

The thread was so fine and taut that Jez could hardly sense it now. She felt an odd lurch inside her, a pleading, but she knew what needed to be done.

I do what I want to, for my own reasons, she said. *And nobody questions me. I'm leader, remember?*

Snap!

It was a physical sensation, the feeling of breaking away, as Morgead was carried off on a wave of his own black anger. He was retreating from her so fast that it made her dizzy. . . .

And then her eyes were open and she was in her own body.

Jez blinked, trying to focus on the room. She was looking up at the ceiling, and everything was too bright and too large and too fuzzy. Morgead's arms were around her and her throat was arched back, still exposed. Every nerve was quivering.

Then suddenly the arms around her let go and she fell. She landed on her back, still blinking, trying to gather herself and figure out which muscles moved what. Her throat stung, and she could feel dampness there. She was giddy.

"What's wrong with you? Get up and get out," Morgead snarled. Jez focused on him. He looked very tall from her upside-down vantage point. His green eyes were as cold as chips of gemstone.

Then she realized what was wrong.

"You took too much blood, you jerk." She tried to put her usual acidity into the words, to cover up her weakness. "It was just supposed to be a ritual thing, but you lost control. I should've known you would."

Something flickered in Morgead's eyes, but then his mouth hardened. "Tough," he said shortly. "You shouldn't have given me the chance."

"I won't make the same mistake again!" She struggled to a sitting position, trying not to show the effort it cost her. The problem—again—was that she wasn't a vampire. She couldn't recover as quickly from loss of blood . . . but Morgead didn't know that.

Not that he'd care, anyway.

Part of her winced at that, tried to argue, but Jez brushed it aside. She needed all her strength and every wall she could build if she was going to get past what had happened.

It *shouldn't* have happened, whatever it had been. It had been some horrible mistake, and she was lucky to have gotten away with her life. And from now on, the only thing to do was try to forget it.

"I probably should tell you why I'm here," she said, and got to her feet without a discernable wobble. "I forgot to mention it before."

"Why you came back? I don't even want to know." He only wanted her to leave; she could tell that from his posture, from the tense way he was pacing.

"You will when I tell you." She didn't have the energy to yell at him the way she wanted. She couldn't afford the luxury of going with her emotions.

"Why do you always think you know what I want?" he snapped, his back to her.

"Okay. Be like that. You probably wouldn't appreciate the chance anyway."

Morgead whirled. He glared at her in a way that meant he could think of too many nasty things to say to settle on one. Finally he just said almost inaudibly, "What chance?"

"I didn't come back just to take over the gang. I want to *do* things with it. I want to make us more powerful."

In the old days the idea would have made him grin, put a wicked sparkle in his eyes. They'd always agreed on power, if nothing else.

Now he just stood there. He stared at her. His expression changed slowly from cold fury to suspicion to dawning insight. His green eyes narrowed, then widened. He let out his breath.

And then he threw back his head and laughed and laughed and laughed.

Jez said nothing, just watched him, inconspicuously testing her balance and feeling relieved that she could stand without fainting. At last, though, she couldn't stand the sound of that laughing anymore. There was very little humor in it.

"Want to share the joke?"

"It's just . . . of course. I should have known. Maybe I *did* know, underneath." He was still chuckling, but it was a vicious noise, and his eyes were distant and full of something like hatred. Maybe self-hatred. Certainly bitterness.

Jez felt a chill.

"There's only one thing that could have brought you back. And I should have realized that from the instant you turned up. It wasn't concern for anybody here; it's got nothing to do with the gang." He looked her straight in the face, his lips curved in a perfect, malevolent smile. He had never been more handsome, or more cold.

"I know what it is, Jez Redfern. I know exactly why you're here today."

CHAPTER

10

Jez held herself perfectly still, keeping her face expressionless. Her mind was clicking through strategies. Two exits—but to go out the window meant a three-story drop, and she probably wouldn't survive that in her condition. Although, of course, she couldn't leave anyway without doing something to silence Morgead—and she wouldn't survive a fight, either. . . .

She suppressed any feeling, returned Morgead's gaze, and said calmly, "And why is that?"

Triumph flashed in his eyes. "Jez *Redfern*. That's the key, isn't it? Your family."

I'll have to kill him somehow, she thought, but he was going on.

"Your family sent you. Hunter Redfern. He knows that I've really found the Wild Power, and he expects you to get it out of me."

Relief spread slowly through Jez, and her stomach muscles relaxed. She didn't let it show. "You idiot! Of course not. I don't run errands for the Council."

Morgead's lip lifted. "I didn't say the Council. I said Hunter Redfern. He's trying to steal a march on the Council, isn't he? He wants the Wild Power himself. To restore the Redferns to the glory of old. You're running errands for *him*."

Jez choked on exasperation. Then she listened to the part of her mind that was telling her to keep her temper and think clearly.

Strategy, that part was saying. He's just *handed* you the answer and you're trying to smack it away.

"All right; what if that is true?" she said at last, her voice curt. "What if I do come from Hunter?"

"Then you can tell him to get bent. I told the Council my terms. I'm not settling for anything less."

"And what were your terms?"

He sneered. "As if you didn't know." When she just stared at him, he shrugged and stopped pacing. "A seat on the Council," he said coolly, arms folded.

Jez burst out laughing. "You," she said, "are out of your mind."

"I know they won't give it to me." He smiled, not a nice smile. "I expect them to offer something like control of San Francisco. And some position after the millennium."

After the millennium. Meaning after the apocalypse, after the human race had been killed or subjugated or eaten or whatever else Hunter Redfern had in mind.

"You want to be a prince in the new world order," Jez said slowly, and she was surprised at how bitterly it came out. She was surprised at how *surprised* she was. Wasn't it just what she expected of Morgead?

"I want what's coming to me. All my life I've had to stand around and watch humans get everything. After the millennium things will be different." He glared at her broodingly.

Jez still felt sick. But she knew what to say now.

"And what makes you think the *Council* is going to be around after the millennium?" She shook her head. "You're better off going with Hunter. I'd bet on him against the Council any day."

Morgead blinked once, lizardlike. "He's planning on getting rid of the Council?"

Jez held his gaze. "What would *you* do in his place?"

Morgead's expression didn't get any sweeter. But she could see from his eyes that she had him.

He turned away sharply and went to glower out the window. Jez could practically see the wheels turning in his head. Finally he looked back.

"All right," he said coldly. "I'll join Hunter's team—but only on my terms. After the millennium—"

"After the millennium you'll get what you deserve." Jez couldn't help glaring back at him. Morgead brought out all her worst traits, all the things she tried to control in herself.

"You'll get a position," she amended, spinning the story she knew he wanted to hear. She was winging it, but she had no choice. "Hunter wants people loyal to him in the new order. And if you can prove you're valuable, he'll want you. But first you have to prove it. Okay? Deal?"

"If I can trust you."

"We can trust each other because we have to. We both want the same thing. If we do what Hunter wants, we both win."

"So we cooperate—for the time being."

"We cooperate—and we see what happens," Jez said evenly.

They stared at each other from opposite sides of the room. It was as if the blood sharing had never happened. They were back to their old roles—maybe a little more hostile, but the same old Jez and Morgead, enjoying being adversaries.

Maybe it'll be easy from now on, Jez thought. As long as Hunter doesn't show up to blow my story.

Then she grinned inwardly. It would never happen. Hunter Redfern hadn't visited the West Coast for fifty years.

"Business," she said crisply, out loud. "Where's the Wild Power, Morgead?"

"I'll show you." He walked over to the futon and sat down.

Jez stayed where she was. "You'll show me what?"

"Show you the Wild Power." There was a TV with a VCR at the foot of the bed, sitting on the bare floor. Morgead was putting a tape in.

Jez settled on the far end of the futon, glad for the chance to sit.

"You've got the Wild Power on *tape?*"

He threw her an icy glance over his shoulder. "Yeah, on *America's Funniest Home Videos.* Just shut up, Jez, and watch."

Jez narrowed her eyes and watched.

What she was looking at was a TV movie about a doomsday asteroid. A movie she'd seen—it had been awful. Suddenly the action was interrupted by the logo of a local news station. A blond anchorwoman came on screen.

"Breaking news in San Francisco this hour. We have live pictures from the Marina district where a five-alarm fire is raging through a government housing project. We go now to Linda Chin, who's on the scene."

The scene switched to a dark-haired reporter.

"Regina, I'm here at Taylor Street, where firefighters are trying to prevent this spectacular blaze from spreading—"

Jez looked from the TV to Morgead. "What's this got to do with the Wild Power? I saw it live. It happened a couple weeks ago. I was watching that stupid movie—"

She broke off, shocked at herself. She'd actually been about to say "I was watching that stupid movie with Claire and Aunt Nan." Just like that, to blurt out the names of the humans she lived with. She clenched her teeth, furious.

She'd already let Morgead know one thing: that

a couple of weeks ago she'd been in this area, where a local news station could break in.

What was *wrong* with her?

Morgead tilted a sardonic glance at her, just to show her that he hadn't missed her slip. But all he said was "Keep watching. You'll see what it's got to do with the Wild Power."

On screen the flames were brilliant orange, dazzling against the background of darkness. So bright that if Jez hadn't known that area of the Marina district well, she wouldn't have been able to tell much about it. In front of the building firefighters in yellow were carrying hoses. Smoke flooded out suddenly as one of the hoses sprayed a straight line of water into the flames.

"Their greatest fear is that there may be a little girl still inside this complex—"

Yes. That was what Jez remembered about this fire. There had been a kid. . . .

"Look here," Morgead said, pointing.

The camera was zooming in on something, bringing the flames in close. A window in the pinky-brown concrete of the building. High up, on the third floor. Flames were pouring up from the walkway below it, making the whole area look too dangerous to approach.

The reporter was still talking, but Jez had tuned her out. She leaned closer, eyes fixed on that window.

Like all the other windows, it was half covered with a wrought-iron screen in a diamond pattern. Unlike the others, it had something else: On the sill there were a couple of plastic buckets with dirt and scraggly plants. A window box.

And a face looking out between the plants.

A child's face.

"There," Morgead said.

The reporter was speaking. "Regina, the fire-fighters say there is definitely someone on the third floor of this building. They are looking for a way to approach the person—the little girl—"

High-powered searchlights had been turned on the flames. That was the only reason the girl was visible at all. Even so, Jez couldn't distinguish any features. The girl was a small blurry blob.

Firefighters were trying to maneuver some kind of ladder toward the building. People were running, appearing and disappearing in the swirling smoke. The scene was eerie, otherworldly.

Jez remembered this, remembered listening to the barely suppressed horror in the reporter's voice, remembered Claire beside her hissing in a sharp breath.

"It's a kid," Claire had said, grabbing Jez's arm and digging her nails in, momentarily forgetting how much she disliked Jez. "Oh, God, a kid."

And I said something like, "It'll be okay," Jez remembered. But I knew it wouldn't be. There was too much fire. There wasn't a chance. . . .

The reporter was saying, "The entire building is involved. . . ." And the camera was going in for a close-up again, and Jez remembered realizing that they were actually going to *show* this girl burning alive on TV.

The plastic buckets were melting. The firemen were trying to do something with the ladder. And then there was a sudden huge burst of orange, an explosion, as the flames below the window *poofed* and began pouring themselves upward with frantic energy. They were so bright they seemed to suck all the light out of their surroundings.

They engulfed the girl's window.

The reporter's voice broke.

Jez remembered Claire gasping, "No . . ." and her nails drawing blood. She remembered wanting to shut her own eyes.

And then, suddenly, the TV screen flickered and a huge wall of smoke billowed out from the building. Black smoke, then gray, then a light gray that looked almost white. Everything was lost in the smoke. When it finally cleared a little, the reporter was staring up at the building in open amazement, forgetting to turn toward the camera.

"This is astonishing. . . . Regina, this is a complete turnaround. . . . The firefighters have—either the water has suddenly taken effect or something else has caused the fire to die. . . . I've never seen anything like this. . . ."

Every window in the building was now belching white smoke. And the picture seemed to have gone washed-out and pale, because there were no more vivid orange flames against the darkness.

The fire was simply gone.

"I really don't know what's happened, Regina. . . . I think I can safely say that everybody here is very thankful. . . ."

The camera zoomed in on the face in the window. It was still difficult to make out features, but Jez could see coffee-colored skin and what seemed to be a calm expression. Then a hand reached out to gently pick up one of the melted plastic buckets and take it inside.

The picture froze. Morgead had hit Pause.

"They never did figure out what stopped the fire. It went out everywhere, all at once, as if it had been smothered."

Jez could see where he was going. "And you think it was some sort of Power that killed it. I don't know, Morgead—it's a pretty big assumption. And to jump from that to the idea that it was a Wild Power—"

"You missed it, then." Morgead sounded smug.

"Missed *what*?"

He was reversing the tape, going back to the moment before the fire went out. "I almost missed it myself when I saw it live. It was lucky I was taping it. When I went back and looked again, I could see it clearly."

The tape was in slow motion now. Jez saw the burst of orange fire, frame by frame, getting larger. She saw it crawl up to engulf the window.

And then there was a flash.

It had only showed up as a flicker at normal speed, easily mistaken for some kind of camera problem. At this speed, though, Jez couldn't mistake it.

It was blue.

It looked like lightning or flame; blue-white with

a halo of more intense blue around it. And it *moved*. It started out small, a circular spot right at the window. In the next frame it was much bigger, spreading out in all directions, fingers reaching into the flames. In the next frame it covered the entire TV screen, seeming to engulf the fire.

In the next frame it was gone and the fire was gone with it. White smoke began to creep out of windows.

Jez was riveted.

"Goddess," she whispered. "Blue fire."

Morgead ran the tape back to play the scene again. " 'In blue fire, the final darkness is banished;/ In blood, the final price is paid.' If that girl isn't a Wild Power, Jez . . . then what is she? You tell me."

"I don't know." Jez bit her lip slowly, watching the strange thing blossom on the TV again. So the blue fire in the poem meant a new kind of energy. "You're beginning to convince me. But—"

"Look, everybody knows that one of the Wild Powers is in San Francisco. One of the old hags in the witch circle—Grandma Harman or somebody— had a dream about it. She saw the blue fire in front of Coit Tower or something. And everybody knows that the four Wild Powers are supposed to start manifesting themselves around now. I think that girl did it for the first time when she realized she was going to die. When she got that desperate."

Jez could picture that kind of desperation; she'd pictured it the first time, when she'd been watching the fire live. How it must feel . . . being trapped like that. Knowing that there was no earthly help for you, that you were about to experience the most terrible pain imaginable. Knowing that you were going to feel your body char and your hair burn like a torch and that it would take two or three endless minutes before you died and the horror was over.

Yeah, you would be desperate, all right. Knowing all that might drag a new power out of you, a frantic burst of strength, like an unconscious scream pulled from the depths of yourself.

But one thing bothered her.

"If this kid is the Wild Power, why didn't her Circle notice what happened? Why didn't she tell them, 'Hey, guys, look; I can put out fires now?'"

Morgead looked annoyed. "What do you mean, her Circle?"

"Well, she's a witch, right? You're not telling me vampires or shapeshifters are developing new powers like *that*."

"Who said anything about witches or vampires or shapeshifters? The kid's *human*."

Jez blinked.

And blinked again, trying to conceal the extent of her astonishment. For a moment she thought Morgead was putting her on, but his green eyes were simply exasperated, not sly.

"The Wild Powers . . . can be human?"

Morgead smiled suddenly—a smirk. "You really didn't know. You haven't heard all the prophecies, have you?" He struck a mocking oratorical pose. "There's supposed to be:

One from the land of kings long forgotten;
One from the hearth which still holds the spark;
One from the Day World where two eyes are
   watching;
One from the twilight to be one with the dark."

The Day World, Jez thought. Not the Night World, the human world. At least one of the Wild Powers had to be human.

Unbelievable . . . but why not? Wild Powers were supposed to be weird.

Then she thought of something and her stomach sank.

"No wonder you're so eager to turn her in," she said softly. "Not just to get a reward—"

"But because the little scum deserves to die—or whatever it is Hunter has in mind for her." Morgead's voice was matter-of-fact. "Yeah, vermin have no right developing Night World powers. Right?"

"Of course right," Jez said without emotion. I'm going to have to watch this kid every minute, she thought. He's got no pity at all for her—Goddess knows what he might do before letting me have her.

"Jez." Morgead's voice was soft, almost pleasant, but it caught Jez's full attention. "Why didn't Hunter tell you that prophecy? The Council dug it up last week."

She glanced at him and felt an inner shiver. Suspicion was cold in the depths of his green eyes. When Morgead was yelling and furious he was dangerous enough, but when he was quiet like this, he was deadly.

"I have no idea," she said flatly, tossing the problem back at him. "Maybe because I was already out here in California when they figured it out. But why don't you call him and ask yourself? I'm sure he'd love to hear from you."

There was a pause. Then Morgead gave her a look of disgust and turned away.

A good bluff is priceless, Jez thought.

It was safe now to move on. She said, "So what do the 'two eyes watching' mean in the prophecy?"

He rolled his own eyes. "How should I know? *You* figure it out. You've always been the smart one."

Despite the heavy sarcasm, Jez felt a different kind of shiver, one of surprise. He really believed that. Morgead was so smart himself—he'd seen that flicker on the TV screen and realized what it was, when apparently none of the adults in the Bay Area had—but he thought she was smarter.

"Well, you seem to be doing all right yourself," she said.

She had been looking steadily at him, to show him no weakness, and she saw his expression change. His green eyes softened slightly, and the sarcastic quirk of his lip straightened.

"Nah, I'm just blundering along," he muttered, his gaze shifting. Then he glanced back up and somehow they were caught in a moment when they were just looking at each other in silence. Neither of them turned away, and Jez's heart gave a strange thump.

The moment stretched.

Idiot! This is ridiculous. A minute ago you were

scared of him—not to mention sickened by his attitude toward humans. You can't just suddenly switch to *this*.

But it was no good. Even the realization that she was in danger of her life didn't help. Jez couldn't think of a thing to say to break the tension, and she couldn't seem to look away from Morgead.

"Jez, look—"

He leaned forward and put a hand on her forearm. He didn't even seem to know he was doing it. His expression was abstracted now, and his eyes were fixed on hers.

His hand was warm. Tingles spread from the place where it touched Jez's skin.

"Jez . . . about before . . . I didn't . . ."

Suddenly Jez's heart was beating far too quickly. I *have* to say something, she thought, fighting to keep her face impassive. But her throat was dry and her mind a humming blank. All she could feel clearly was the place where she and Morgead touched. All she could see clearly was his eyes. Cat's eyes, deepest emerald, with shifting green lights in them. . . .

"Jez," he said a third time.

And Jez realized all at once that the silver thread between them hadn't been broken. That it might be stretched almost into invisibility, but it was still *there*, still pulling, trying to make her body go weak and her vision blur. Trying to make her fall toward Morgead even as he was falling toward her.

And then came the sound of someone kicking in the front door.

CHAPTER

11

"Hey, Morgead!" the voice was shouting even as the door went slamming and crashing open, sticking every few inches because it was old and warped and didn't fit the frame anymore.

Jez had jerked around at the first noise. The connection between her and Morgead was disrupted, although she could feel faint echoes of the silver thread, like a guitar string vibrating after it was strummed.

"Hey, Morgead—"

"Hey, you still asleep—?" Several laughing, raucous people were crowding into the room. But the yelling stopped abruptly as they caught sight of Jez.

There was a gasp, and then silence.

Jez stood up to face them. She couldn't afford to feel tired anymore; every muscle was lightly tensed, every sense alert.

She knew the danger she was in.

Just like Morgead, they were the flotsam and jet-sam of the San Francisco streets. The orphans, the ones who lived with indifferent relatives, the ones nobody in the Night World really wanted. The for-gotten ones.

Her gang.

They were out of school and ready to rumble.

Jez had always thought, from the day she and Morgead began picking these kids up, that the Night World was making a mistake in treating them like garbage. They might be young; they might not have families, but they had power. Every one of them had the strength to be a formidable opponent.

And right now they were looking at her like a group of wolves looking at dinner. If they all de-cided to go for her at once, she would be in trouble. Somebody would end up getting killed.

She faced them squarely, outwardly calm, as a quiet voice finally broke the silence.

"It's really you, Jez."

And then another voice, from beside Jez. "Yeah, she came back," Morgead said carelessly. "She joined the gang again."

Jez shot him the briefest of sideways glances. She hadn't expected him to help. He returned the look with an unreadable expression.

". . . she came back?" somebody said blankly.

Jez felt a twinge of amused sympathy. "That's right," she said, keeping her face grave. "I had to go away for a while, and I can't tell you where, but now I'm back. I just fought my way back in—and I beat Morgead for the leadership." She figured she might as well get it all over with at once. She had no idea how they were going to react to the idea of her as leader.

There was another long moment of silence, and then a whoop. A sound that resembled a war cry. At the same instant there was a violent rush toward Jez—four people all throwing themselves at her. For a heartbeat she stood frozen, ready to fend off a four-fold attack.

Then arms wrapped around her waist.

"Jez! I missed you!"

Someone slapped her on the back almost hard enough to knock her down. "You bad girl! You beat him *again*?"

People were trying to hug her and punch her and pat her all at once. Jez had to struggle not to show she was overwhelmed. She hadn't expected this of them.

"It's good to see you guys again," she said. Her voice was very slightly unsteady. And it was the truth.

Raven Mandril said, "You scared us when you disappeared, you know." Raven was the tall, willowy one with the marble-pale skin. Her black hair was short in back and long in front, falling over one eye and obscuring it. The other eye, midnight blue, gleamed at Jez.

Jez allowed herself to gleam back, just a bit. She had always liked Raven, who was the most mature of the group. "Sorry, girl."

"*I* wasn't scared." That was Thistle, still hugging Jez's waist. Thistle Galena was the delicate one who had stopped her aging when she reached ten. She was as old as the others, but tiny and almost weightless. She had feathery blond hair, amethyst eyes, and little glistening white teeth. Her specialty was playing the lost child and then attacking any humans who tried to help her.

"You're never scared," Jez told her, squeezing back.

"She means she knew you were all right, wherever you were. I did, too," Pierce Holt said. Pierce was the slender, cold boy, the one with the aristocratic face and the artist's hands. He had dark blond hair and deep-set eyes and he seemed to carry his own windchill factor with him. But just now he was looking at Jez with cool approval.

"I'm glad somebody thought so," Jez said, with a glance at Morgead, who just looked condescending.

"Yeah, well, *some* people were going crazy. They thought you were dead," Valerian Stillman put in, following Jez's look. Val was the big, heroic one, with deep russet hair, gray-flecked eyes, and the build of a linebacker. He was usually either laughing or yelling with impatience. "Morgead had us scouring the streets for you from Daly City to the Golden Gate Bridge—"

"Because I was hoping a few of you would fall off," Morgead said without emotion. "But I had no such luck. Now shut up, Val. We don't have time for all this class-reunion stuff. We've got something important to do."

Thistle's face lit up as she stepped back from Jez. "You mean a hunt?"

"He means the Wild Power," Raven said. Her one visible eye was fixed on Jez. "He's told you already, hasn't he?"

"I didn't need to tell her," Morgead said. "She already knew. She came back because Hunter Redfern wants to make a deal with us. The Wild Power for a place with him after the millennium."

He got a reaction—the one Jez knew he expected. Thistle squeaked with pleasure, Raven laughed huskily, Pierce gave one of his cold smiles, and Val roared.

"He knows we've got the real thing! He doesn't wanna mess with us!" he shouted.

"That's right, Val; I'm sure he's quaking in his boots," Morgead said. He glanced at Jez and rolled his eyes.

Jez couldn't help but grin. This really was like old times: she and Morgead trading secret looks about Val. There was a strange warmth sweeping through her—not the scary tingling heat she'd experienced with Morgead alone, but something simpler. A feeling of being with people who liked her and knew her. A feeling of belonging.

She never felt that at her human school. She'd seen things that would drive her human classmates insane even to imagine. None of them had any idea of what the real world was like—or what Jez was like, for that matter.

But now she was surrounded by people who understood her. And it felt so good that it was alarming.

She hadn't expected this, that she would slip back into the gang like a hand in a glove. Or that something inside her would look around and sigh and say, "We're home."

Because I am *not* home, she told herself sternly. These are not my people. They don't really know me, either. . . .

But they don't have to, the little sigh returned. You don't ever need to tell them you're human. There's no reason for them to find out.

Jez shoved the thought away, scrunched down hard on the sighing part of her mind. And hoped it would stay scrunched. She tried to focus on what the others were saying.

Thistle was talking to Morgead, showing all her small teeth as she smiled. "So if you've got the terms settled, does that mean we get to do it now? We get to pick the little girl up?"

"Today? Yeah, I guess we could." Morgead looked at Jez. "We know her name and everything. It's Iona Skelton, and she's living just a couple buildings down from where the fire was. Thistle made friends with her earlier this week."

Jez was startled, although she kept her expression relaxed. She hadn't expected things to move this fast. But it might all work out for the best, she realized, her mind turning over possibilities quickly. If she could snatch the kid and take her back to Hugh, this whole masquerade could be over by tomorrow. She might even live through it.

"Don't get too excited," she warned Thistle, combing some bits of grass out of the smaller girl's silk-floss hair. "Hunter wants the Wild Power alive and unharmed. He's got plans for her."

"Plus, before we take her, we've got to test her," Morgead said.

Jez controlled an urge to swallow, went on combing Thistle's hair with her fingers. "What do you mean, test her?"

"I'd think that would be obvious. We can't take the chance of sending Hunter a dud. We have to make sure she *is* the Wild Power."

Jez raised an eyebrow. "I thought you *were* sure," she said, but of course she knew Morgead was right. She herself would have insisted Hugh find a way to test the little girl before doing anything else with her.

The problem was that Morgead's testing was likely to be . . . unpleasant.

"I'm sure, but I still want to test her!" Morgead snapped. "Do you have a problem with that?"

"Only if it's dangerous. For us, I mean. After all, she's got some kind of power beyond imagining, right?"

"And she's in elementary school. I hardly think she's gonna be able to take on six vampires."

The others were looking back and forth between Morgead and Jez like fans at a tennis match.

"It's just as if she never left," Raven said dryly, and Val bellowed laughter while Thistle giggled.

"They always sound so—married," Pierce observed, with just a tinge of spite to his cold voice.

Jez glared at them, aware that Morgead was doing the same. "I wouldn't marry him if every other guy on earth was dead," she informed Pierce.

"If it were a choice between her and a human, I'd pick the human," Morgead put in nastily.

Everyone laughed at that. Even Jez.

The sun glittered on the water at the Marina. On Jez's left was a wide strip of green grass, where people were flying huge and colorful kites, complicated ones with dozens of rainbow tails. On the sidewalk people were Rollerblading and jogging and walking dogs. Everybody was wearing summer clothing; everybody was happy.

It was different on the other side of the street.

Everything changed over there. A line of pinky-brown concrete stood like a wall to mark the difference. There was a high school and then rows of a housing project, all the buildings identically square, flat, and ugly. And on the next street beyond them, there was nobody walking at all.

Jez let Morgead take the lead on his motorcycle as he headed for those buildings. She always found this place depressing.

He pulled into a narrow alley beside a store with a dilapidated sign proclaiming "Shellfish De Lish." Val roared in after him, then Jez, then Raven with Thistle riding pillion behind her, and finally Pierce. They all turned off their motors.

"That's where she lives now; across the street," Morgead said. "She and her mom are staying with her aunt. Nobody plays in the playground; it's too dangerous. But Thistle might be able to get her to come down the stairs."

"Of course I can," Thistle said calmly. She showed her pointed teeth in a grin.

"Then we can grab her and be gone before her mom even notices," Morgead said. "We can take her back to my place and do the test where it's private."

Jez breathed once to calm the knot in her stomach. "*I'll* grab her," she said. At least that way she might be able to whisper something comforting to the kid. "Thistle, you try to get her right out to the sidewalk. Everybody else, stay behind me—if she sees a bunch of motorcycles, she'll probably freak. But be ready to gun it when I pull out and grab her. The noise should help cover up any screams. Raven, you pick up Thistle as soon as I get the kid, and we all go straight back to Morgead's."

Everyone was nodding, looking pleased with the plan—except Morgead.

"I think we should knock her out when we grab her. That way there won't *be* any screams. Not to mention any blue fire when she figures out she's being kidnapped—"

"I already said how we're going to do it," Jez cut in flatly. "I don't want her knocked out, and I don't think she'll be able to hurt us. Now, everybody get ready. Off you go, Thistle."

As Thistle skipped across the street, Morgead let out a sharp breath. His jaw was tight.

"You never could take advice, Jez."

"And you never could take orders." She could see

him starting to sizzle, but only out of the corner of her eye. Most of her attention was focused on the housing building.

It was such a desolate place. No graffiti—but no grass, either. A couple of dispirited trees in front. And that playground with a blue metal slide and a few motorcycles-on-springs to ride . . . all looking new and untouched.

"Imagine growing up in a place like this," she said.

Pierce laughed oddly. "You sound as if you feel sorry for her."

Jez glanced back. There was no sympathy in his deep-set dark eyes—and none in Raven's midnight blue or Val's hazel ones, either. Funny, she didn't remember them being *that* heartless—but of course she hadn't been sensitive to the issue back in the old days. She would never have stopped to wonder about what they felt for human children.

"It's because it's a kid," Morgead said brusquely. "It's hard on any kid growing up in a place like this."

Jez glanced at him, surprised. She saw in his emerald green eyes what she'd missed in the others; a kind of bleak pity. Then he shrugged, and the expression was gone.

Partly to change the subject, and partly because she was curious, she said, "Morgead? Do you know the prophecy with the line about the blind Maiden's vision?"

"What, this one?" He quoted:

"Four to stand between the light and the
shadow,
Four of blue fire, power in their blood.
Born in the year of the blind Maiden's vision;
Four less one and darkness triumphs."

"Yeah. What do you think 'born in the year of
the blind Maiden's vision' *means*?"

He looked impatient. "Well, the Maiden has to
be Aradia, right?"

"Who's that?" Val interrupted, his linebacker
body quivering with interest.

Morgead gave Jez one of his humoring-Val looks.
"The Maiden of the Witches," he said. "You know,
the blind girl? The Maiden part of the Maiden,
Mother, and Crone group that rules all the witches?
She's only one of the most important people in the
Night World—"

"Oh, yeah. I remember." Val settled back.

"I agree," Jez said. "The blind Maiden has to be
Aradia. But what does the 'year of her vision'
mean? How old is this kid we're snatching?"

"About eight, I think."

"Did Aradia have some special vision eight
years ago?"

Morgead was staring across the street, now, his
eyebrows together. "How should I know? She's
been having visions since she went blind, right?
Which means, like, seventeen years' worth of 'em.
Who's supposed to tell which one the poem
means?"

"What *you* mean is that you haven't even tried to figure it out," Jez said acidly.

He threw her an evil glance. "You're so smart; you do it."

Jez said nothing, but she made up her mind to do just that. For some reason, the poem bothered her. Aradia was eighteen now, and had been having visions since she lost her sight at the age of one. Some particular vision must have been special. Otherwise, why would it be included in the prophecy?

It had to be important. And part of Jez's mind was worried about it.

Just then she saw movement across the street. A brown metal door was opening and two small figures were coming out.

One with feathery blond hair, the other with tiny dark braids. They were hand in hand.

Something twisted inside Jez.

Just stay calm, *stay calm*, she told herself. It's no good to think about grabbing her and making a run for the East Bay. They'll just follow you; track you down. Stay cool and you'll be able to get the kid free later.

Yeah, after Morgead does his little "test."

But she stayed cool and didn't move, breathing slowly and evenly as Thistle led the other girl down the stairs. When they reached the sidewalk, Jez pressed the starter button.

She didn't say "Now!" She didn't need to. She just peeled out, knowing the others would follow like a flock of well-trained ducklings. She heard their engines roar to life, sensed them behind her in tight formation, and she headed straight for the sidewalk.

The Wild Power kid wasn't dumb. When she saw Jez's motorcycle coming at her, she tried to run. Her mistake was that she tried to save Thistle, too. She tried to pull the little blond girl with her, but Thistle was suddenly strong, grabbing the chain-link fence with a small hand like steel, holding them both in place.

Jez swooped in and caught her target neatly around the waist. She swooped the child onto the saddle facing her, felt the small body thud against her, felt hands clutch at her automatically for balance.

Then she whipped past a parked car, twisted the throttle to get a surge of speed, and flew out of there.

Behind her, she knew Raven was snagging Thistle and the others were all following. There wasn't a scream or even a sound from the housing project.

They were roaring down Taylor Street. They were passing the high school. They were making it away clean.

"Hang on to me or you'll fall off and get hurt!" Jez yelled to the child in front of her, making a turn so fast that her knee almost scraped the ground. She wanted to stay far enough ahead of the others that she could talk.

"Take me back home!" The kid yelled it, but not hysterically. She hadn't shrieked even once. Jez looked down at her.

And found herself staring into deep, velvety brown eyes. Solemn eyes. They looked reproachful and unhappy—but not afraid.

Jez was startled.

She'd expected crying, terror, anger. But she had the feeling that this kid wouldn't even be yelling if it hadn't been the only way to be heard.

Maybe I should have been more worried about what she'll do to us. Maybe she can *call blue fire down to kill people. Otherwise, how can she be so composed when she's just been kidnapped?*

But those brown eyes—they weren't the eyes of somebody about to attack. They were—Jez didn't know what they were. But they wrenched her heart.

"Look—Iona, right? That's your name?"

The kid nodded.

"Look, Iona, I know this seems weird and scary—having somebody just grab you off the street. And I can't explain everything now. But I promise you, you're not going to get hurt. Nothing's going to hurt you—okay?"

"I want to go home."

Oh, kid, so do I, Jez thought suddenly. She had to blink hard. "I'm going to take you home—or at least someplace safe," she added, as honesty unexpectedly kicked in. There was something about the kid that made her not want to lie. "But first we've got to go to a friend of mine's house. But, look, no matter how strange all this seems, I want you to remember something. I won't let you get hurt. Okay? Can you believe that?"

"My mom is going to be scared."

Jez took a deep breath and headed onto the freeway. "I promise I won't let you get hurt," she said again. And that was all she could say.

She felt like a centaur, some creature that was half person and half steel horse, carrying off a human kid at sixty miles an hour. It was pointless to try to make conversation on the freeway, and Iona didn't speak again until they were roaring up to Morgead's building.

Then she said simply, "I don't want to go in there."

"It's not a bad place," Jez said, braking front and back. "We're going up on the roof. There's a little garden there."

A tiny flicker of interest showed in the solemn brown eyes. Four other bikes pulled in beside Jez.

"Yeeehaw! We got her!" Val yelled, pulling off his helmet.

"Yeah, and we'd better take her upstairs before somebody sees us," Raven said, tossing her dark hair so it fell over one eye again.

Thistle was climbing off the back of Raven's motorcycle. Jez felt the small body in front of her stiffen. Thistle looked at Iona and smiled her sharp-toothed smile.

Iona just looked back. She didn't say a word, but after a minute Thistle flushed and turned away.

"So now we're going to test her, right? It's time to test her, isn't it, Morgead?"

Jez had never heard Thistle's voice so shrill—so

disturbed. She glanced down at the child in front of her, but Morgead was speaking.

"Yeah, it's time to test her," he said, sounding unexpectedly tired for somebody who'd just pulled off such a triumph. Who'd just caught a Wild Power that was going to make his career. "Let's get it over with."

CHAPTER

12

Jez kept one hand on the kid as they walked up the stairs under the dirty fluorescent bulbs. She could only imagine what Iona must be thinking as they shepherded her to the top.

They came out on the roof into slanting afternoon sunlight. Jez gave Iona's shoulder a little squeeze.

"See—there's the garden." She nodded toward a potted palm and three wooden barrels with miscellaneous wilted leaves in them. Iona glanced that way, then gave Jez a sober look.

"They're not getting enough water," she said as quietly as she said everything.

"Yeah, well, it didn't rain enough this summer," Morgead said. "You want to fix that?"

Iona just looked seriously at him.

"Look, what I mean is, you've got the Power, right? So if you just want to show us right now, anything you want, be my guest. It'll make things a lot simpler. Make it rain, why don't you?"

Iona looked right at him. "I don't know what you're talking about."

"I'm just saying that there's no reason for you to get hurt here. We just want to see you do something like what you did the night of the fire. Anything. Just show us."

Jez watched him. There was something incongruous about the scene: Morgead in his high boots and leather jacket, iron-muscled, sleek, sinewy, on one knee in front of this harmless-looking kid in pink pants. And the kid just looking back at him with her sad and distant eyes.

"I guess you're crazy," Iona said softly. Her pigtails moved as she shook her head. A pink ribbon fluttered loosely.

"Do you remember the fire?" Jez said from behind her.

"Course." The kid turned slowly around. "I was scared."

"But you didn't get hurt. The fire got close to you and then you did something. And then the fire went away."

"I was scared, and then the fire went away. But I didn't do anything."

"Okay," Morgead said. He stood. "Maybe if you can't tell us, you can show us."

Before Jez could say anything, he was picking up the little girl up and carrying her. He had to step over a line of debris that stretched like a diagonal wall from one side of the roof to the other. It was composed of telephone books, splintery logs, old clothes, and other odds and ends, and it formed a barrier, blocking off a corner of the roof from the rest.

He put Iona in the triangle beyond the debris. Then he stepped back over the wall, leaving her there. Iona didn't say anything, didn't try to follow him back out of the triangle.

Jez stood tensely. The kid's a Wild Power, she told herself. She's already survived worse than this. And no matter what happens, she's not going to get hurt.

I promised her that.

But she would have liked to be telepathic again just for a few minutes, just to tell the kid one more time not to be scared. She especially wanted to as Val and Raven poured gasoline on the wall of debris. Iona watched them do it with huge sober eyes, still not moving.

Then Pierce lit a match.

The flames leaped up yellow and blue. Not the bright orange they would have been at night.

But hot. They spread fast and Jez could feel the heat from where she was standing, ten feet away.

The kid was closer.

She still didn't say anything, didn't try to jump over the flames while they were low. In a few moments they were high enough that she couldn't jump through them without setting herself on fire.

Okay, Jez thought, knowing the kid couldn't hear her. Now, *do it!* Come on, Iona. Put the fire out.

Iona just looked at it.

She was standing absolutely still, with her little hands curled into fists at her sides. A small and lonely figure, with the late afternoon sun making a soft red halo around her head and the hot wind from the fire rippling her pink-trimmed shirt. She faced the flames dead-on, but not aggressively, not as if she were planning to fight them.

Damn; this is *wrong*, Jez thought. Her own hands were clenched into fists so tightly that her nails were biting into her palms.

"You know, I'm concerned," Pierce said softly from just behind her. "I have a concern here."

Jez glanced at him quickly. Pierce didn't talk a lot, and he always seemed the coldest of the group—aside from Morgead, of course, who could be colder than anyone. Now Jez wondered. Could he, who never seemed to be moved by pity, actually be the most sensitive?

"I'm worried about this fire. I know nobody can look down on us, but it's making a lot of smoke. What if one of the other tenants comes up to investigate?"

Jez almost hit him.

This is *not* my home, she thought, and felt the part of her that had sighed and felt loved and understood wither away. These are not my people. I don't belong with them.

And Pierce wasn't worth hitting. She turned her back on him to look at Iona again. She was dimly aware of Morgead telling him to shut up, that other tenants were the least of their worries, but most of her attention was focused on the kid.

Come on, kid! she thought. Then she said it out loud.

"Come on, Iona! Put out the fire. You can do it! Just do what you did before!" She tried to catch the child's eye, but Iona was looking at the flames. She seemed to be trembling now.

"Yeah, come on!" Morgead said brusquely. "Let's get this over with, kid."

Raven leaned forward, her long front hair ruffling in the wind. "Do you remember what you did that night?" she shouted seriously. "Think!"

Iona looked at her and spoke for the first time. "I didn't do anything!" Her voice, so composed before, was edging on tears.

The fire was full-blown now, loud as a roaring wind, sending little bits of burning debris into the air. One floated down to rest at Iona's foot and she stepped backward.

She's got to be scared, Jez told herself. That's the whole point of this test. If she's not scared, she'll never be able to find her Power. And we're talking about saving the world, here. We're not just torturing this kid for fun. . . .

It's still wrong.

The thought burst out from some deep part of her. Jez had seen a lot of horrible things as a vampire and a vampire hunter, but suddenly she knew she couldn't watch any more of *this*.

I'm going to call it off.

She looked at Morgead. He was standing tensely, arms folded over his chest, green eyes fixed on Iona as if he could will her into doing what he wanted. Raven and Val were beside him, Raven expressionless under her fall of dark hair; Val frowning with his big hands on his hips. Thistle was a step or so behind them.

"It's time to stop," Jez said.

Morgead's head whipped around to look at her. "No. We've gotten this far; it would be stupid to have to start all over again. Would that be any nicer to her?"

"I said, it's time to *stop*. What do you have to put out the fire—or did you even think of that?"

As they were talking, Thistle stepped forward. She moved right up to the flames, staring at Iona.

"You'd better do something fast," she shouted. "Or you're going to burn right up."

The childish, taunting tone caught Jez's attention, but Morgead was talking to her.

"She's going to put it out any minute now. She just has to be frightened enough—"

"Morgead, she's absolutely terrified already! Look at her!"

Morgead turned. Iona's clenched fists were now raised to chest-level; her mouth was slightly open as she breathed far too fast. And although she wasn't screaming or crying like a normal kid, Jez could see the tremors running through her little body. She looked like a small trapped animal.

"If she's not doing it now, she's never going to,"

Jez told Morgead flatly. "It was a stupid idea in the first place, and it's over!"

She saw the change in his green eyes; the flare of anger and then the sudden darkness of defeat. She realized that he was going to cave.

But before he could say anything, Thistle moved forward.

"You're gonna die!" she shrilled. "You're gonna burn up right now!" And she began kicking flaming debris at Iona.

Everything happened very fast after that.

The debris came apart in a shower of sparks as it flew toward Iona. Iona's mouth came open in horror as she found fiery garbage swirling around her knees. And then Raven was yelling at Thistle, but Thistle was already kicking more.

A second deluge of sparks hit Iona. Jez saw her put up her hands to protect her face, then fling her arms out as a piece of burning cloth settled on her sleeve. She saw the sleeve spurt with a tiny flame. She saw Iona cast a frantic look around, searching for a way to escape.

Morgead was dragging Thistle back by her collar. Thistle was still kicking. Sparks were everywhere and Jez felt a hot pain on her cheek.

And then Iona's eyes went enormous and blank and fixed and Jez could see that she'd made some decision, she'd found some way to get out of this.

Only not the right one.

She was going to jump.

Jez saw Iona turn toward the edge of the roof,

and she knew in that same instant that she couldn't get to the child in time to stop her.

So there was only one thing to do.

Jez only hoped she would be fast enough.

She very nearly wasn't. But there was a two-foot wall at the roof's perimeter, and it delayed Iona for a second as she scrambled onto it. That gave Jez a second to leap through the fire and catch up.

And then Iona was on the wall, and then she was launching her small body into empty space. She jumped like a flying squirrel, arms and legs outspread, looking down at the three-story drop.

Jez jumped with her.

Jez! The telepathic shout followed her, but Jez scarcely heard it. She had no idea who had even said it. Her entire consciousness was focused on Iona.

Maybe some part of her was still hoping that the kid had magic and could make the wind hold her up. But it didn't happen and Jez didn't waste time thinking about it. She hit Iona in midair, grabbing the small body and hanging on.

It was something no human could have done. Jez's vampire muscles instinctively knew how to handle this, though. They twisted her as she fell, putting her underneath the child in her arms, putting her legs below her like a cat's.

But of course Jez didn't have a vampire's resistance to injury. She knew perfectly well that when she hit, the fall would break both her legs. In her weakened state it might well kill her.

It should save the kid, though, she thought unemotionally as the ground rushed up to meet her. The extra resiliency of Jez's flesh would act as a cushion.

But there was one thing Jez hadn't thought of.

The trees.

There were discouraged-looking redbud trees planted at regular intervals along the cracked and mossy sidewalk. None of them had too much in the way of foliage even in late summer, but they certainly had a lot of little branches.

Jez and the kid crashed right into one of them.

Jez felt pain, but scratching, stabbing pain instead of the slamming agony of hitting the sidewalk. Her legs were smashing through things that cracked and snapped and poked her. Twigs and branches. She was being flipped around as some of the twigs caught on her jeans and others snagged her leather jacket. Every branch she hit decreased her velocity.

So when she finally crashed out of the tree and hit concrete, it merely knocked the wind out of her.

Black dots danced in front of her eyes. Then her vision cleared and she realized that she was lying on her back with Iona clutched to her stomach. Shiny redbud leaves were floating down all around her.

Goddess, she thought. We made it. I don't believe it.

There was a dark blur and something thudded against the sidewalk beside her.

Morgead. He landed like a cat, bending his knees, but like a *big* cat. A three-story jump was pretty steep even for a vampire. Jez could see the shock reverberate through him as his legs hit concrete, and then he fell forward.

That must hurt, she thought with distant sympathy. But the next instant he was up again, he was by her side and bending over her.

"Are you all right?" He was yelling it both aloud and telepathically. His dark hair was mussed and flying; his green eyes were wild. *"Jez!"*

Oh. It was you who yelled when I jumped, Jez thought. I should have known.

She blinked up at him. "Of course I'm all right," she said hazily. She tugged at the kid lying on her. "Iona! Are *you* all right?"

Iona stirred. Both her hands were clutching Jez's jacket in front, but she sat up a little without letting go. There was a burned patch on her sleeve, but no fire.

Her velvety brown eyes were huge—and misty. She looked sad and confused.

"That was really scary," she said.

"I know." Jez gulped. She wasn't any good at talking about emotional things, but right now the words spilled out without conscious effort. "I'm sorry, Iona; I'm so sorry, I'm so sorry. We shouldn't have done that. It was a very bad thing to do, and I'm really sorry, and we're going to take you home now. Nobody's going to hurt you. We're going to take you back to your mom."

The velvety eyes were still unhappy. Tired and unhappy and reproachful. Jez had never felt like more of a monster; not even that night in Muir

Woods when she had realized she was hunting her own kind.

Iona's gaze remained steady, but her chin quivered.

Jez looked at Morgead. "Can you erase her memory? I can't see any reason why she should have to remember all this."

He was still breathing quickly, his face pale and his pupils dilated. But he looked at Iona and nodded. "Yeah, I can wipe her."

"Because she's not the Wild Power, you know," Jez said levelly, as if making a comment about the weather.

Morgead flinched. Then he shoved his hair back with his knuckles, his eyes shutting briefly.

"She's an extraordinary kid, and I don't know exactly what she's going to be—maybe President or some great doctor or botanist or something. Something special, because she's got that inner light—something that keeps her from getting mad or mean or hysterical. But that's got nothing to do with being a Wild Power."

"All right! I know, already!" Morgead yelled, and Jez realized she was babbling. She shut up.

Morgead took a breath and put his hand down. "She's not it. I was wrong. I made a bad mistake. Okay?"

"Okay." Jez felt calmer now. "So can you please wipe her?"

"Yes! I'm doing it!" Morgead put his hands on Iona's slender shoulders. "Look, kid, I'm—sorry. I never thought you'd—you know, jump like that."

Iona didn't say anything. If he wanted forgiveness, he wasn't getting it.

He took a deep breath and went on. "This has been a pretty rotten day, hasn't it? So why don't you just forget all about it, and before you know it, you'll be home."

Jez could feel him reach out with his mind, touching the child's consciousness with his Power. Iona's eyes shifted, she looked at Jez uncertainly.

"It's okay," Jez whispered. "It won't hurt." She hung on to Iona's gaze, trying to comfort her as Morgead's suggestions took hold.

"You don't ever have to remember this," Morgead said, his voice soothing now. Gentle. "So why don't you just go to sleep? You can have a little nap . . . and when you wake up, you'll be home."

Iona's eyelids were closing. At the last possible second she gave Jez a tiny sleepy smile—just the barest change of expression, but it seemed to ease the tightness in Jez's chest. And then Iona's lashes were lying heavy on her cheeks and her breathing was deep and regular.

Jez sat up and gently put the sleeping child on the sidewalk. She smoothed back one stray pigtail and watched the little chest rise and fall a couple of times. Then she looked up at Morgead.

"Thanks."

He shrugged, exhaling sharply. "It was the least I could do." Then he gave her an odd glance.

Jez thought of it at the same instant. She was the one so concerned about the child—why had she asked Morgead to wipe her memory?

Because I can't do it, she thought dryly. Out loud she said, "I'm really kind of tired, after everything that's happened today. I don't have much Power left."

"Yeah . . ." But his green eyes were slightly narrowed, searching.

"Plus, I hurt." Jez stretched, gingerly testing her muscles, feeling every part of her protest.

The searching look vanished instantly. Morgead leaned forward and began to go over her with light, expert fingers, his eyes worried.

"Can you move everything? What about your legs? Do you feel numb anywhere?"

"I can move everything, and I only wish I felt numb somewhere."

"Jez—I'm sorry." He blurted it out as awkwardly as he had to the child. "I didn't mean . . . I mean, this just hasn't turned out the way I planned. The kid getting hurt—you getting hurt. It just wasn't what I had in mind."

The kid getting hurt? Jez thought. Don't tell me you care about that.

But there was no reason for Morgead to lie. And he did look unhappy—probably more unhappy than Jez had ever seen him. His eyes were still all pupil, as if he were scared.

"I'm not hurt," Jez said. It was all she could think of. She felt dizzy suddenly—uncertain and a little giddy, as if she were still tumbling off the roof.

"Yes, you are." He said it with automatic stubbornness, as if it were one of their arguments. But his hand reached out to touch her cheek.

The one that had been hit by burning debris. It hurt, but Morgead was touching so lightly. . . . Coolness seemed to flow from his fingers, seeping into the burn and making it feel better.

Jez gasped. "Morgead—what are you doing?"

"Giving you some Power. You're low and you need it."

Giving her Power? She'd never heard of such a thing. But he was *doing* it. She could feel her skin healing itself faster, could feel his strength pour into her.

It was a strange sensation. It made her shiver inwardly.

"Morgead . . ."

His eyes were fixed on her face. And suddenly they were all Jez could see; the rest of the world was a blur. All she could hear was the soft catch in his breath; all she could feel was the gentleness of his touch.

"Jez . . ."

They were leaning toward each other, or falling. It was that silver thread between them, shortening, pulling. They had nothing to grab on to but each other. And then Morgead's arms were around her and she felt his warm mouth touch hers.

CHAPTER

13

The kiss was warm and sweet. Not frightening. Jez felt herself relax in Morgead's arms before she knew what she was doing. His heart was beating so fast against hers. She felt dizzy, but safe, too; a wonderful feeling.

But the approach of his mind was another thing. It was just like the first time: that terrible, irresistible pull trying to suck her soul out and mix it with Morgead's until they were both one person. Until he knew her every secret and she had no place to hide.

And the worst thing was that she knew it wasn't Morgead doing it. It was that outside force doing it to both of them, carrying them along helplessly.

Whether we want it or not. And we *don't* want it, Jez told herself desperately. We both hate it. Neither of us wants to share our souls. . . .

But then why was he still holding her, still kissing her? And why was she letting him?

At that instant she felt his mind touch hers, reaching through the smoke-screen of protection she'd thrown around herself to brush her thoughts as lightly as a moth's wing. She recognized Morgead's essence in it; she could feel his soul, dark and bright and full of fierce emotion for her. He was opening himself to her; not trying to fight this or even holding back. He was going farther than the pull forced him to, giving himself to her freely. . . .

It was a gift that sent her reeling. And she couldn't resist it. Her mind flowed out of its own accord to touch his, tendrils of thought wrapping around his gratefully. The shock of pleasure when she let it happen was frightening—except that she couldn't be frightened anymore, not now.

And then she felt him respond, felt his happiness, felt his thoughts enfolding hers, holding her mind as gently as his arms held her body. And white light exploded behind her eyes. . . .

Jez! Morgead! What's wrong with you two?
The thought was foreign, cold, and unwanted. It broke into Jez's warm little world and rattled around annoyingly. Jez tried to push it away.

Hey, look; I'm just trying to help. If you guys are alive, then, like give us a sign, okay?
Morgead made a sound like a mental groan. *It's Val. I have to kill him.*

I'm going to help, Jez told him. Then something occurred to her. *Oh—wait. Where are we . . . ?*

It was a good question. A weird but necessary question. It took them a moment to untangle their thoughts from each other and rise back to the real world.

Where they seemed to be sitting under the ruins of a redbud tree, arms around each other, Jez's head on Morgead's shoulder, Morgead's face pressed into Jez's hair.

At least we weren't still kissing, Jez thought abstractedly. She could feel herself flushing scarlet. The rest of the gang was standing around them, looking down with worried expressions.

"What do you guys want?" Morgead said brusquely.

"What do we *want?*" Raven leaned forward, dark hair swinging. Jez actually saw both her midnight blue eyes underneath. "You three jumped off the roof just as the fire got out of control. We put it out and came down to see if you were still alive— and then we find you here hanging on to each other and totally out of it. And you want to know what we *want?* We want to know if you're *okay.*"

"We're fine," Morgead said. He didn't say anything more, and Jez understood. Neither of them had any desire to talk about it in front of other people. That could wait until they were alone, until it was the right time.

They didn't need to express this to each other. Jez simply knew, and knew that he knew.

"What about *her?*" Thistle pointed to Iona, still asleep on the sidewalk.

Jez was already moving to the child. She checked the little body over, noted the even breathing and the peaceful expression.

"She's fine, too," she said, settling back. She held Thistle's gaze. "No thanks to you."

Thistle's cheeks were pink. She looked angry, embarrassed, and defensive. "She's just a human."

"She's a kid!" Morgead yelled, shooting up to his feet. He towered over Thistle, who suddenly looked very small. "Which *you're* not," he went on unsympathetically. "You're just a—a sixteen-year-old Shirley Temple-wannabe."

"All right, both of you!" Jez said sharply. She waited until they shut up and looked at her before continuing. "You—be quiet and let me take care of things," she said to Morgead. "And *you*—if you ever try to hurt a kid again, I'll knock your head off." This to Thistle, who opened her mouth, but then shut it again without speaking.

Jez nodded. "Okay, that's settled. Now we've got to get this girl home."

Val stared at her. "Home?"

"Yeah, Val." Jez picked the child up. "In case you missed something, she's not the Wild Power."

"But . . ." Val wriggled his broad shoulders uncomfortably and looked at Morgead. "You mean you were wrong?"

"There's a first time for everything, right?" Morgead glared at him.

"But, then—who *is* the Wild Power?" Raven put in quietly.

"Who knows?" It was the first time Pierce had spoken, and his voice was low and distantly amused.

Jez glanced at him. His blond hair glinted in the red light of the sunset, and his dark eyes were mocking.

I really don't think I like you much, she thought.

But of course he was right. "If this kid isn't the one—well, I guess it could have been anybody at the scene," she said slowly. "Anybody worried enough to want to save her. One of the firefighters, a neighbor—anybody."

"Assuming the blue flash on the tape really was evidence of a Wild Power," Pierce said.

"I think it was." Jez glanced at Morgead. "It sure looked like blue fire. And it certainly was some kind of Power."

"And Grandma Harman dreamed about the Wild Power being in San Francisco," Morgead added. "It all fits too well." He looked at Jez slyly. "But it couldn't have been anybody at the scene, you know."

"Why not?"

"Because of what you said about that line in the prophecy. 'Born in the year of the blind Maiden's vision.' That means it has to be somebody born less than eighteen years ago. Before that, Aradia couldn't have visions because she wasn't alive."

Goddess, I'm slow today, Jez thought. I should have thought of that. She gave him a wry nod of respect and he returned it with a grin. Not maliciously.

"It's still not much to go on," Raven said in her pragmatic way. "But don't you think we should go back inside to discuss it? Somebody's going to come along eventually and see us with an unconscious kid."

"Good point," Jez said. "But I'm not going up with you. I'm taking the kid home."

"Me, too," Morgead said. Jez glanced at him; he had his stubborn expression on.

"Okay, but just us. Two motorcycles are going to be conspicuous enough." She turned to Raven. "The rest of you can do what you want tonight; try to figure out who the Wild Power is or whatever. We'll meet again tomorrow and see what we've come up with."

"Why wait?" Val said. "It's only dusk. We could meet tonight—"

"I'm tired," Jez cut in. "It's enough for the day." *And* Goddess knows how I'm going to explain being gone *this* long to Aunt Nan, she thought wearily. Not to mention missing school.

Pierce was watching her with an odd expression. "So you'll have to report to Hunter that we failed," he said, and there was a probing tone in his voice that Jez didn't like.

"Yeah, I'll tell him you screwed up," she said heavily. "But that we still have some options. Unless you'd rather I just tell him that you're all idiots and not worth giving a second chance." She kept looking at Pierce until he looked away.

When she turned to Morgead he was scowling, but he didn't say anything. He silently started toward their bikes.

They couldn't talk while they were riding. Jez was too full of her own thoughts anyway.

She was finally free to consider those last minutes with Morgead.

It had been . . . amazing. Electrifying. But also enlightening.

She knew now what had happened to them, what was happening. He had been right. It was the soulmate principle.

So we're soulmates. Morgead and I. After all our fighting and challenging each other and everything. It's so strange, but in a way it makes sense, too. . . .

And it's really a pity that even if we both survive the next week or so, we're never going to see each other again.

The thought came from some deep part of her that was utterly heartless and practical and saw everything in the cold light of truth.

Because unfortunately the universe had picked the wrong person for Jez to be soulmates with. It had picked one that would hate her and want to kill her once he realized what she really was.

Bad mistake, universe, Jez thought, biting down on a laugh. She realized, dimly, that she was verging on being hysterical.

It had been such a long day, and she was so tired, and so hurt, and she'd failed in her mission, and now Morgead was in love with her, but there was just no hope. Small wonder she was punchy and an emotional wreck. She was lucky not to be falling off her bike.

There really was no hope. Even in that last encounter, even when Morgead had been revealing his soul to her, Jez had managed to keep her own secrets buried. He didn't know. He had no idea that the girl he was in love with was vermin. Was working with Circle Daybreak. Was lying to him to steal the Wild Power out from under his nose and end the hopes of the vampires for a world without humans.

He was ambitious, she had always known that. All he'd ever cared about was climbing higher and getting more power. She'd promised him a position in the new world order—while all the time she was working as hard as she could to make sure that the new world order never came.

He would never forgive that deception. He would never even be able to understand why she had done it.

So you have to forget about him, the cold-and-practical part of her mind said quietly. And there was nothing inside Jez that even tried to argue.

It was dark by the time they reached the Marina district. As they approached the housing project, Jez saw flashing lights ahead.

Police car lights. Well, that wasn't unexpected. Iona's mother would have notified them by now. Jez just hoped she wasn't too worried. . . .

Idiot! her mind said sarcastically. How worried do you expect her to be, with it getting dark and her eight-year-old missing?

She turned into an alley and Morgead followed her.

"We'll have to do a drive-by," she said over the thrum of the engines. "Drop her by the police cars and then shoot out of there. They'll probably chase us. Are you up for it?"

He nodded. "We should go separate ways. That'll make it harder for them to catch us."

"Right. You go on home once you lose them. So will I."

She couldn't see his features clearly in the dark alley, but she knew he was looking at her. "So will you? Go home?"

"I mean I'll go to the place where I'm staying."

She expected him to ask about that, try to find out where it was, what she was doing. He didn't. Instead he said, "Do you have to?"

She blinked at him, startled. Then she frowned. "Yes, I have to. I *want* to. I'm tired, Morgead, and anyway I'm not ready to be spending the night with a guy."

"I didn't mean that—"

Jez waved a hand. "I know. I'm sorry. But I'm still tired, and—" And I've got other responsibilities that you don't understand. And if I stick around you any longer, while I'm this tired, I'm afraid that you're going to find out what they are.

"And you're still mad," he said bleakly.

"I'm not mad—"

"Or disgusted or whatever."

What was he talking about? "I'm just tired," she

said firmly. "Now let's drop the kid off, and I'll see you tomorrow."

"I—" He let out his breath violently. "All right."

Jez didn't waste any more time. She unzipped her jacket, which had been holding Iona firmly against her. Then she sped out into the street.

One block, two blocks. And now she was right beside the dark and deserted playground, and now she was almost level with the police cars. There were several officers standing around talking, and several other bystanders who might be neighbors.

Jez targeted one of the neighbors.

She swooped in toward the woman, who was on the outside edge of the sidewalk. She came up fast, then hit the brakes.

"Hey," she said. "Here."

The woman turned around and her jaw dropped. Jez didn't hesitate, just bundled Iona into her arms. The woman grabbed the child's weight automatically.

"Give her to her mom, okay?"

And then Jez was roaring out and away. She could hear Morgead behind her, and shouts from the housing project. Then a police siren.

She glanced back. Morgead was just turning on a side street. He waved once at her, and then he was speeding off.

Jez could hear more sirens now. She twisted the throttle and headed for the Bay Bridge.

At least a pursuit was something she could enjoy.

When she finally shook the police cars tailing her, she turned toward Clayton. She would have been worried about what her aunt and uncle were going to say if she hadn't already been too worried about Iona.

She'll be all right, she told herself. She shouldn't remember anything, and her mom will take care of her.

But Jez couldn't help but feel guilty . . . and just plain sad. There was some sort of bond between her and the child. She felt—responsible for her, and not just because she'd kidnapped and terrorized her.

Nobody should have to grow up in that kind of place. I may have run around on the streets when I was little, but at least I had Uncle Bracken, and a nice home to go to if I wanted. Iona—she doesn't even have a safe playground.

I should do something for her, but what can I do that would matter?

I don't know; maybe I can visit her sometime. Maybe I can buy her a plant. . . .

There weren't any easy answers, and she was drawing up to a neat yellow frame house.

Home.

Time, Jez thought, to face the music. Uncle Jim and Aunt Nan and nasty little Claire. She just hoped they left enough of her alive so that she could call Hugh afterward.

She pulled her motorcycle into the garage, climbed off, and went inside.

". . . at all is bad enough. But to do it the day after you make us a promise—well, what are we supposed to think? How are we supposed to trust you again?"

Jez was sitting on the blue floral couch in the living room. The Goddard living room didn't get used much, only for very formal occasions.

This was one of them. It was a court martial.

And there wasn't really a thing that Jez could say to the humans she lived with. She certainly couldn't give them any excuse that would make sense.

"First, ditching Claire even though you swore to us that you'd let her drive you to school." Aunt Nanami was ticking items off on her fingers. "Second, ditching school after you swore to us you weren't going to skip again. Third, going off some place you won't even tell us about. Fourth, not even calling to let us know you were still alive. Fifth, getting home at almost ten o'clock at night—"

Uncle Jim cleared his throat. "Nan, I think we've been over this already."

A couple of times, Jez thought. Oh, well, at least Claire is enjoying it. Her cousin was standing at the entrance to the living room, openly listening. When she happened to catch Jez's eye she smiled brilliantly, her small face actually glowing with smug satisfaction.

Aunt Nan was shaking her head. "I just want to make sure she *understands*, Jim. I thought she understood last night, but obviously . . ." She threw her hands up.

"Well, the thing is—" Uncle Jim cleared his throat again and looked at Jez. He looked uncomfortable; he wasn't very good at discipline, but Jez could see that he'd reached his limit. "The thing is that we can't just keep yelling at you. We have to *do* something, Jez. So we've decided to lock up your motorcycle. You can't ride it anymore, not until you learn to be more responsible."

Jez sat stunned.

Not her bike. They couldn't take her bike from her. How would she *get* anywhere?

She had to be mobile. She had to get to Morgead tomorrow—she had to get to *Hugh* sometime. She had to be able to track down the Wild Power. And she couldn't do any of that without transportation.

But she could see from Uncle Jim's face that he was serious. He'd finally decided to put his foot down, and Jez had gotten caught underneath it.

She let out her breath. Part of her wanted to yell and storm and rage about this, to lose control and make a big noisy fuss.

But it wouldn't do any good. Besides, she'd managed to keep her temper for almost a year with these people, to live her double life as a student and vampire hunter and make it all work. To blow that now would be stupid.

And another part of her was scared that she was even verging on losing control. That was what even a day with Morgead did to her. It cut through all her careful discipline and changed her back into a raving barbarian.

Morgead . . . she couldn't think about him now.

"Okay, Uncle Jim," she said out loud. "I understand. You do what you have to."

"If you can just show us that you're learning to

be responsible, then you can have the bike back. You have to learn to take life more seriously, Jez."

That forced a tired snort out of her. She was laughing before she knew it, and her aunt and uncle were looking shocked and displeased.

"I'm sorry," she said. "I'll try harder."

And I'll just have to take public transportation tomorrow, she thought when the lecture was over and she was free to go to her room. Even though that's a lot more dangerous. I could get hunted down so easily. . . .

"You messed with the wrong person, you know?" Claire said as Jez reached her door. "You shouldn't have dumped me like that. You shouldn't make me mad."

"Yeah, Claire; well, now I know better. I'm terrified."

"You're *still* not taking things seriously, are you?"

"Claire—" Jez rounded on the smaller girl. Then she stopped dead. "I don't have time for this," she muttered. "I have to make a call. You just run along and harass somebody else."

She shut the bedroom door in Claire's face.

Which, she realized later, was a mistake. At the time, though, she was too tired to think about it.

She was too tired to think properly at all. Tired and distraught, with the feeling that everything was closing in and happening too fast.

And so when she picked up the phone to dial Hugh she hardly noticed the little click on the line, and she didn't stop for even a second to consider what it meant.

CHAPTER
14

"**D**id you have trouble getting away?" Hugh said.

It was the next morning, a very different sort of day from yesterday. The sky was overcast and the air was heavy. Everyone Jez had passed at the Concord BART station looked a little depressed.

"Eh, a little," she said, and sat down by Hugh on the platform. They were at the far end of the station, beyond the covered area with benches, beside a little concrete security house. It was a safe and private meeting place since the station was almost deserted after the morning commute. "They chained up my bike with this huge chain. Claire drove me to school—she's been watching me like a werewolf guarding dinner. And Aunt Nan called the office to make sure I didn't cut."

Hugh shifted in concern. There was a tiny breath

of warm wind, and it stirred his fair hair. "So what did you do?"

Jez grinned. "I cut." She shrugged and added, "I got a guy from my auto shop class to drive me here. It wasn't hard."

He smiled at her sadly, his gray eyes distant. "But they're going to find out. Jez, I'm really sorry for completely messing up your life."

She shrugged again. "Yeah, but if I don't do it, everybody's life is going to be even more completely messed up. Every human's."

"I know." He shivered slightly. Then he drew up his legs, clasping his arms around them. He looked at her with his chin on his knees. "So what did you find out?"

"That the girl Morgead thought was the Wild Power isn't." He looks so cute that way, Jez thought helplessly. So—compact. Morgead would never sit like that.

Hugh winced. "Great. You're sure?"

"Yeah. It was a little kid, eight years old, and she was something special—but not that. She was . . ." Jez tried to think of a way to describe it. Hugh watched her with eyes that were clear and fathomless, sad and wry and gentle all at once. And suddenly Jez got it. She gasped.

"Goddess—I know! She was like *you*. That kid was an Old Soul."

Hugh's eyebrows went up. "You think?"

"I'm sure of it. She had that same way of looking at you as if she's seen all of history and she knows that you're just a little part. That . . . 'big picture' look. As if she were beyond stupid human things."

"But not a Wild Power," Hugh said softly. He looked half discouraged and half relieved. "So then the Morgead connection is useless."

"Actually, no. Because he's got evidence for the Wild Power on videotape." Jez explained about the movie and the fire and the blue flash. "So somebody around that kid is probably it. I know that area and so does Morgead. We may be able to find out who."

Hugh chewed his lip. Then he looked directly at her. "It sounds dangerous. Just how is Morgead taking this—you coming back and all?"

Jez stared out across the BART tracks. They looked like regular train tracks, except for the big one labeled DANGER ELECTRIC THIRD RAIL. There was a sound like faraway thunder, and then a train came whizzing up like a sleek futuristic white dragon. It stopped and a few people got on and off in the distance. She waited until it left again to answer.

"He . . . wasn't very happy at first. But then he kind of got used to it. I don't think he's going to make any trouble—unless he finds out, you know."

She wasn't sure what else to say. She didn't want to talk to Hugh about Morgead—and she certainly didn't want to explain what had happened. Especially not when she was so confused about it all herself.

"You still think he'd hate you if he found out you were half human?" Hugh's voice was quiet.

Jez laughed shortly. "Believe it. He would."

There was a silence, while Hugh looked at her. Suddenly Jez found her mind posing an odd question. If it were Hugh or Morgead, which would she take?

Of course, it was a completely *ridiculous* question. She couldn't have either of them. Hugh was an Old Soul, and beyond her reach. Not to mention that he only thought of her as a friend. And Morgead might be her soulmate, but he would murder her if he ever discovered the truth.

But still, if she did have a choice . . . Hugh or Morgead?

A day ago she'd have said Hugh without question. How strange that now it came up the other way.

Because, impossible as it was, deadly as she knew it to be, it was Morgead she was in love with. And she had only just understood that this moment.

What a pity that there was no hope in the world for them.

Jez found herself giving another short laugh—and then she realized that Hugh was still looking at her. She could feel color rise to her cheeks.

"You were miles away again."

"I'm just foggy. Not enough sleep, I guess." Plus all that fun yesterday. She was still sore from the stick fight and the fall with Iona. But that wasn't Hugh's problem.

She took a breath, groping for another subject. "You know, there was something I wanted to ask you. Morgead said the Council had dug up another prophecy—about where each of the Wild Powers is from. Have you heard it?" When he shook his head, she quoted:

"One from the land of kings long forgotten;
One from the hearth which still holds the spark;
One from the Day World where two eyes are
    watching;
One from the twilight to be one with the dark."

"Interesting." Hugh's gray eyes had lit up. " 'One from the hearth' . . . that's got to be the Harman witches. Their last name was originally 'Hearth-Woman.' "

"Yeah. But the line about the one from the Day World—that one's a human, right?"

"It sounds like it."

"That's what Morgead thought—that's why he thought the little girl might be a Wild Power even though she was human. But what I can't figure out is what it means by 'where two eyes are watching.' "

"Mmm . . ." Hugh gazed into the distance, as if he liked the challenge. "The only thing I can think of that combines the idea of 'Day' and 'eyes' is a poem. It goes something like 'The Night has a thousand eyes, and the Day only one.' The one eye being the sun, you know, and the thousand eyes the stars at night."

"Hmpf. What about the moon?"

Hugh grinned. "I don't know. Maybe the author wasn't good at astronomy."

"Well—that doesn't help much. I thought it might be a clue. But the truth is that we don't even know if it's the human Wild Power we're after."

Hugh put his chin on his knees again. "True. But I'll let Circle Daybreak know about that prophecy. It might help eventually." He was silent a moment, then added, "You know, they dug up something interesting, too. Apparently the Hopi Tribe predicted the end of the world pretty accurately."

"The Hopi?"

"I should say, the ends of the worlds. They knew that it had happened before their time, and that it would happen again. Their legend says that the first world was destroyed by fire. The second world was destroyed by ice. The third world ended in water—a universal flood. And the fourth world—well, that's ours. It's supposed to end in blood and darkness—and end soon."

Jez murmured, "The first world—?"

"Don't remember your Night World history?" He *tched* at her, with a smile that didn't reach his eyes. "The first civilization was the shapeshifters'. Back when humans were scared to go out of their caves, the shapeshifters ruled and the humans thought of them as gods. Animal spirits, totems. It was Shapeshifter World. That lasted for about ten thousand years, until a bunch of volcanoes suddenly became active—"

"Fire."

"Yeah. The weather changed, people migrated, and the shapeshifters lost control. After that it was really Witch World. The witches did better than everybody else for ten thousand years, but then there was an Ice Age—"

"And the Night Wars," Jez said, remembering. "When the vampires fought the witches."

"Right. And after all that, the vampires were in control; it was Vampire World. Which lasted about another ten thousand years, until the flood. And after the flood, human civilization really started. It was Human World, and it has been for a long time. The Night People have just been hanging on around the edges, hiding. But . . ." He paused and straightened. "That started about eight thousand B.C."

"Oh."

"Yeah. The millennium marks the end of our ten thousand years." He gave his gentle, half-mocking smile. "We humans are about to lose our lease. Something's going to happen to bring blood and darkness and then there'll be a whole new world."

"Only if we don't stop it," Jez said. "And we will—because we have to."

Hugh's smiled changed, softening. "I think we're lucky to have people like you trying." Then he lost the smile completely. He looked uncertain. "Jez—you know, Old Souls aren't really beyond 'stupid human things.' We're as human as anybody. And we . . . I mean, and I . . ."

Jez's heart was beating uncomfortably fast. The way he was looking at her—she'd never seen Hugh look like that at anything or anyone.

Another rumble in the distance, and then a train came rushing in.

Hugh blinked, glanced up at the digital clock display above the platform, then checked his watch. He cursed.

"I'm supposed to be somewhere. I'm late."

Jez's heart gave a strange thump. But not of disappointment. Weirdly, it was more like relief.

"Me, too," she said. "I'm supposed to meet Morgead before everybody else gets out of school. I ought to take the next train to San Francisco."

He still hesitated. "Jez—"

"Go on," she said, standing up. "I'll call you if I turn up anything. Wish me luck."

"Be careful," he said instead, and then he was hurrying away.

Jez watched him go. She couldn't help wondering what he had been about to say.

Then she turned to walk back to the central part of the station. She was partway around the concrete guardhouse when she heard a noise on the other side.

A stealthy, sneaking noise. Not the kind a security guard would make.

Jez didn't hesitate. Smoothly, completely soundless herself, she changed course, turning back and going around the structure the other way to get behind the sneaker. The instant she had a clear view of the intruder's back, she jumped.

She landed on top of her quarry, with a control hold on the person's wrist. But she already knew that this wasn't going to be a fight to the death.

"Jez—ow—it's me!" Claire spluttered.

"I know it's you, Claire."

"Let go of my arm!"

"I don't think so, Claire. You having an interesting morning? Hear any good jokes?"

"Jez!" Claire struggled, hurting herself, then got mad and hurt herself more trying to hit Jez. Jez allowed her to sit up, still keeping hold of her.

Claire's face was flushed and wrathful, her dark hair sticking in strands to her cheeks. Her eyes were shooting sparks.

"Okay, so I'm sorry for eavesdropping. I followed you when Greg Ludlum drove you here. I wanted to know what you were doing. I didn't know that you were completely freaking insane!"

"Well, it's too bad you didn't figure it out earlier. Because unfortunately I have to kill you now to keep you from talking."

Claire's eyes widened and she choked. Jez suddenly realized that underneath all the sparks and the yelling her cousin was terrified.

She let go of Claire's arm and Claire slumped away from her, rubbing it.

"You—you *are* insane, aren't you?" Claire looked at her sideways, through clinging strands of hair. "I mean, all that stuff about the world ending—it's some kind of bizarre game you're playing with your weird friends, isn't it? Some kind of Dungeons and Dragons stuff . . ."

"What do you think, Claire?" Jez stood up and offered Claire a hand, worried that someone might notice them. She kept that hand on Claire as she herded Claire back behind the guard house.

The truth was that this situation wasn't funny.

Claire really was in trouble—because Jez was in trouble.

Her entire cover was blown. Everything she'd worked for in the past year—Claire could destroy it all. Claire knew way too much, and Claire hated her enough to use it.

"I think . . . I don't know what to think." Claire swallowed. "Who was that guy?"

"One of my weird friends. Right?"

"He didn't seem so weird. When he said things— I don't know. They sounded . . ." Claire's voice trailed off. Finally it came back, almost inaudibly. "Real."

"Great." *I am going to have to kill her. What else can I do?*

"It's not a game, is it?" Claire said, looking at her. All the anger was gone from the dark eyes now. They were simply bewildered and frightened.

Then Claire shook her head. "But, I mean, it's impossible. Vampires and shapeshifters and witches—it's all just . . ." Her voice trailed off again.

Jez was simply looking at her, with eyes that might be less silvery than a year ago, but that she knew were still pretty strange. And after a few moments Claire's gaze lost its focus and her whole body seemed to fall in on itself, as if it had lost something vital. Innocence maybe, Jez thought grimly.

"Oh, God, it *is* true," Claire whispered. "I mean, it's *really true*. That's why you're gone all the time, isn't it? You're off—doing something."

Jez said, "Yeah."

Claire sagged against the guardhouse. "Oh, God. I . . . God. I feel so strange. It's like—nothing is what I thought."

Yeah, I know the feeling, Jez thought. When the whole world turns around and you have to adjust in two seconds flat. It happened to me, too, a year ago.

But none of that was going to help Claire. All she could say was "I'm sorry."

Claire didn't seem to hear her. She was speaking in a voice that was just a breath. "That's why . . . that's why all that weird stuff with your father. Nobody knowing anything about his family and all. I knew from the beginning that there was something about you; I just couldn't tell what it was."

Oh, great, Jez thought. Here it comes. She tried to keep her face impassive as Claire faced her squarely, raising her eyes with a look somewhere between wonder and dread.

"That guy—he said you were only half human. Which means you're half . . . something else?"

"I'm half human and half vampire," Jez said quietly. The interesting thing was that it was so easy to get out. She'd only ever spoken the words aloud to one person before: Hugh.

Now she looked to see if Claire would actually faint or just fall down.

Claire did neither. She just shut her eyes. "You know the really insane thing? I believe that." She opened her eyes again. "But—I didn't know you *could* be. Half and half."

"Neither did anybody else, till I was born. I'm the

only one." Jez examined her cousin, realized that she really wasn't going to faint. When she spoke again, her voice came out more challenging than she meant it to. "So now that you know, Claire, what are you going to do about it?"

"What do you mean, what am I going to do?" Claire glanced around, then her voice dropped as her eyes glinted with interest. "Look—do you, like, have to drink blood and everything?"

"Not anymore," Jez said shortly. What was this? Who would have thought that studious, straitlaced Claire would have such an interest in vampires?

"But you mean you used to?"

"Before I came to live with you guys. I thought I was a full vampire then. But I found out that I could live without it, as long as I didn't use my powers."

"You've got powers? Really? What kind?"

"No kind. Look, enough with the questions. I told you, I'm not a vampire anymore."

"And you're not evil." Claire said it flatly.

Jez looked at her, startled. "What makes you say *that*?"

"I heard what you were talking about, saving the world and all. I didn't understand it, but it sounded like you were on the right side. And—" Claire hesitated, then shrugged. "And I know *you*, okay? I mean, you're arrogant and stubborn and you never explain anything, but you're not *evil*. You just aren't—inside. I can tell."

Jez laughed. A real laugh. She couldn't help it.

Of all people, Claire. She'd misjudged this girl

who was her own age but had nothing else in common with her. Her cousin had unexpected depths.

"Well, thanks," she said. "I try not to be too evil—these days." Then she sobered. "Look, Claire, if you really think that, and if you really believe that the stuff you heard was true—"

"About the end of the world? I don't believe it. I mean, I heard it, and I believe you believe it—and when I first heard it I kind of believed it, but—"

"Just—skip the rest and plain believe it, Claire. It happens to be the truth. And I'm trying to do something about it."

"Something about a Wild Power, right?" Claire wasn't sagging anymore. She looked almost excited. "But what's a—"

"You don't need to know. The point is that if you want to, you can help me."

"I can? Really?"

"You can help me by going back to school and forgetting that this ever happened. You can help me by keeping my secret and not ever saying a word about this to anybody. And, incidentally, you'll be keeping your family safe at the same time."

Claire looked away, worked her jaw. "This stuff you're doing is pretty dangerous." It wasn't a question.

"Very dangerous." Jez stepped back. "And I'm late for it right now. So do we have a deal? Will you help me or not? Can I trust you?"

"Or otherwise you're gonna kill me, right?" Claire looked at her sarcastically.

Jez rolled her eyes. "Don't tempt me. Seriously, are you going to help?"

"No."

Jez froze, looking down at the shorter girl. *"What?"*

"Jez—don't get mad, but I don't think I *can*. Not that way." Claire was looking back up steadily, her small face serious and surprisingly determined. "I mean how can I possibly just walk away, after hearing all that? If everything you said is true, how can I *forget?*"

"You can because you have to. We all do what we have to do." Jez looked around the station. Another train should be coming any minute. She simply didn't have time to spend convincing a human to stay out of business that would kill her. To properly explain it to Claire would take days.

All she could do was ask for something she never would have imagined Claire could give her.

"Claire . . . there's no way I can convince you or *make* you do what I want. But I'm asking you—" She let out her breath and went on: "I'm asking you to trust me. I'm asking you to walk away and at least try to forget this. And to believe that *I'm* trying the best I can to do the right thing."

Claire kept looking at her steadily for a moment. Then, all at once, the dark eyes filled. They turned away, and Claire's throat moved once as she swallowed. Then, slowly, she nodded.

"Okay," she whispered. "I mean—it's okay for now. I mean, I guess I can talk to you later about it."

Jez let out her breath. "That's right."

Claire stood there for another second, then straightened her shoulders and turned away. But just as suddenly she turned back, looking tense and almost explosive. "There's something I have to say to you."

Jez glanced down the tracks. No train. "Okay."

"It's—it's . . . that I'm sorry. I'm sorry I bugged you and tried to get Mom mad at you and everything. I was just—I was jealous because they let you get away with anything, and . . ." She shook her head fiercely and then went on, shrugging grimly as if she hated to admit it. "And, yeah, because you're so gorgeous and confident and everything. It made me feel bad and I wanted to hurt you. So. Anyway. There. I'm sorry."

She started to walk away, wobbling a little.

"Claire."

Claire paused, then turned around.

Jez spoke a little hesitantly around the obstruction in her throat. "It's okay. And thank you."

"Yeah." Claire grinned and gave a little shrug. "See ya later." She turned around and started walking again.

See ya, Jez thought. She felt suddenly tired and strangely emotional. There was too much inside her: sadness and relief and worry and a new feeling for Claire. She crossed her arms and looked around the station, trying to relax, taking deep, even breaths.

And saw two werewolves coming straight for Claire.

Jez recognized them immediately—not the individuals, but the type. They were 'wolves, and they were thugs. Somebody's hired muscle.

She didn't have her stick, but she didn't need it. She could feel a dangerous smile come to her lips; part anticipation and part sheer fury. Suddenly she wasn't tired, wasn't sore, wasn't anything but perfectly in tune with her body and dying to use it as a weapon.

She launched herself like a streak of red lightning, passing Claire easily and knocking the human girl flat before landing in front of the 'wolves. A guy and a girl. They snapped to attention in front of her, each dropping into a fighting stance.

Behind her, she could hear Claire say, *"Ow."*

"Good morning and welcome to the Bay Area,"

Jez told the 'wolves; then she snap-kicked the girl in the face.

The girl flew backward. She wasn't out of commission, but it had wrecked the joint attack they had been about to make. The guy knew this, but he was a 'wolf, so instead of waiting for his partner to recover, he growled and threw himself at Jez.

Oh, Goddess, this is too easy. As he drove a punch at her face, Jez turned sideways and let his fist whistle past her. Then she threw her left arm around his left hip, holding him in what was almost an embrace. A deadly one, though. At the same instant she slammed her left hand up to his chin, striking with enough force to stun him.

He staggered in her arms, snarling. Bristly hairs erupted on his face.

"Sweet dreams, Fido," Jez said. She hooked her left leg around his right just below the knee and brought him crashing to the platform. His head hit the concrete and he went limp.

Somewhere behind Jez, a sort of thin shrieking had begun. Claire. Jez ignored it, and ignored the two or three people scrambling for the stairs—avoiding the down escalator because it was right beside Jez. She was focused on the female werewolf, who was back on her feet.

"Do yourself a favor and don't even try anything," she said, grinning. "You're way outclassed."

The girl, who had reddish-brown hair and a feral expression, didn't answer. She simply showed her teeth and lunged for Jez.

With both hands reaching for Jez's face. You'd

think they would *learn*, Jez thought. Especially after what just happened.

Even as she was thinking it, her body was making the right moves. She grabbed the girl's leading arm with both hands, then twisted, pulling her off balance. She took the girl down with a pull drop, flipping her to the platform. As soon as the girl was flat Jez locked the arm she still held and began to apply leverage against the elbow joint.

"Don't move or I'll break your elbow," she said pleasantly. The girl was writhing in pain, spitting and struggling and hurting herself worse.

Absently, Jez noticed that Claire had stopped shrieking. She glanced up to make sure her cousin was all right and saw that Claire was on her feet, staring openmouthed. Jez gave her a reassuring nod.

Then she looked back at the female 'wolf. Now that the fight was over she had the leisure to wonder what was going *on*. There were plenty of people who might want to kill her, but she couldn't think of any reason for them to target Claire. And they *had* been targeting her; Jez was sure of that.

This was no random thing. This was two 'wolves attacking a human right in public, in front of witnesses, as if they didn't care who saw them. This was something planned, something important.

She gave the girl's arm a little twist, and the girl snarled wildly, glaring at Jez with reddish eyes full of animal fury and hatred.

"Okay, you know what I want," Jez said. "I need answers, and I don't have much time. What are you doing here? Who sent you? And why do you want *her?*" She jerked her head toward Claire.

The girl just glared harder. Jez applied more pressure.

"Look, I can *make* time for this if I need to. I can do this all day. After I break this elbow I'll do the other one. And then I'll break your ribs, and then your kneecaps—"

"Filthy halfbreed scum," the werewolf snarled.

Jez's heart gave an odd lurch.

She tried to quiet it. Well, now, that was interesting. Somebody obviously knew her secret. And since they'd been going for Claire, they knew Claire was connected with her. . . .

They knew about her family.

Jez saw white light. She threw sudden pressure against the 'wolf's elbow joint. The girl screamed, a sound more of anger than of pain.

"Who hired you?" Jez said softly, each word coming out like a chip of ice. "Who sent you after my cousin?"

She stared into the reddish eyes, trying to reach into the girl's soul and yank an answer out of her.

"Nobody messes with my family," she whispered. "Whoever sent you is going to be sorry."

She couldn't ever remember feeling so angry. And she was so focused on the girl, so intent, that it wasn't until Claire screamed that she realized someone was approaching behind her.

"Jez, watch out!"

The yell woke Jez up. Without releasing her hold on the female 'wolf, she turned around—just in time to see a male vampire stalking her. He must have come up the down escalator.

And behind *him*, unbelievably, was Claire, running and getting ready for a flying tackle.

"Claire, don't!" Jez yelled. She struck the female 'wolf once, with deadly accuracy, on the side of the jaw to knock her out. Then she sprang toward the vampire.

But Claire was already grabbing him—a completely futile and foolish gesture. He whipped around and seized a handful of dark hair, and then he was holding Claire in a choke hold, putting her body between him and Jez.

"One more step and I'll break her neck," he warned.

Jez skidded to a stop.

"You let go of my *cousin*," she spat.

"No, I really think we need to talk first," he said, the beginnings of an ugly grin on his face. "You're the one who's going to give answers—"

Jez kicked him.

A roundhouse kick to his knees while he was busy talking. She didn't worry about keeping it nonlethal. She only cared about breaking his hold on Claire.

It worked. He lost his grip, stumbling sideways. Jez grabbed Claire and thrust her out of the way, shouting "Run! The escalator's right there!"

But Claire didn't run. "I want to help you!"

"Idiot!" Jez didn't have time to say that Claire *couldn't* help her; could only hurt her. The vampire had recovered and was moving toward her in fighting position.

He was big, probably over two hundred pounds. And he was a full vampire, which gave him the advantage of strength and speed. And he was smarter than the 'wolves; he wasn't just going to lunge. And Jez didn't have a weapon.

"Just keep behind me, okay?" she snarled under her breath to Claire.

The vampire grinned at that. He knew Jez was vulnerable. She was going to have to keep half her attention on protecting Claire.

And then, just as he was about to make an attack, Jez heard the smack of footsteps on concrete. Running footsteps, with a weird little hesitation between them, like somebody with a limp. . . .

She flashed a look toward the stairs. Hugh had just rounded the top. He was out of breath and bleeding from cuts on his face. But as soon as he saw her and the vampire he waved his arms and yelled.

"Hey! Ugly Undead! Your friend missed me! You want to have a try?"

Hugh? Jez thought in disbelief. Fighting?

"Come on, hey; I'm here; I'm easy." Hugh was hopping toward the vampire, who was also flashing looks at him, trying to assess this new danger while not taking his focus off Jez.

"You want to go a few rounds?" Hugh dropped into a boxer's pose, throwing punches at the air. "Huh? You want to try for the title?" All the time he was speaking, he was dancing closer to the vampire, circling to get behind him.

Beautiful, Jez thought. All she needed was for the vampire to shift his attention for one second—just to glance behind him once—and she could kick his face in.

It didn't work that way. Something went wrong.

The vampire tried to glance behind him. Jez saw her chance and made the kick, a high kick that snapped his head back. But somehow instead of falling backward the vampire managed to blunder forward straight at her. She could easily have gotten away—except for Claire.

Claire had obediently kept behind her—even when behind her meant standing right by the BART tracks, on the yellow metal squares that marked the edge of the platform. Now, as the vampire stumbled forward and Jez began to slide out of the way, she heard Claire gasp, felt Claire clutch at her wildly.

She knew what had happened instantly. Claire had tried to run the wrong way and was teetering on the edge of the platform. More, she was taking Jez with her.

There was a distant rumble like thunder.

Jez knew she could save herself—by getting rid of Claire. She could use Claire's body as a springboard to propel herself away from the drop. That way, only one of them would die.

Instead, she tried to twist and throw Claire away from her, toward safety. It didn't work. They both lost their balance. Jez had the strange, surprised feeling one gets in the middle of a fall—where's the ground?—and then she hit it.

It was a bad fall because she was tangled with Claire. All Jez could do was try to keep Claire away from the third rail on the far side of the track. The impact winded both of them and Jez saw stars.

She could hear Hugh screaming her name.

The distant thunder had become a roaring, whizzing sound, carried through the tracks underneath Jez. Down here, she could feel a rattling that wasn't audible from above. It was a noise that filled her head and shook her body.

She knew absolutely, in that instant, that they were going to die.

Both of them. Crushed to pieces under the train. The white dragon would run right over them and not even know it.

There was simply no chance. Claire was clinging to her desperately, clawing Jez's arms hard enough to draw blood, and gasping in the breath for a scream. And even if Jez had been a full vampire, she couldn't have lifted Claire the four feet to the platform fast enough.

There was nothing to save them, no hope. No rescue. It was over.

All of this flashed through Jez's mind in the single instant it took her to look up and see the train bearing down on them. Its sleek white nose was only thirty feet away, and it was braking, but nowhere near fast enough, and this was it, the actual moment of her death, the last thoughts she would ever think, and the last thing she would ever see was white, white, white—

Blue.

It happened all at once, filling her vision. One second she could see clearly, the next the entire world was blue. Not just blue. Fiery, dazzling, lightning-shot blue. Like being inside some sort of science-fiction special effect. There was blue streaming and crackling and sizzling all around her, a cocoon of blue that enfolded her and shot past her and disappeared somewhere ahead.

I'm dead, Jez thought. So *this* is what it's like. Completely different from what people say.

Then she realized that she could hear a faint shrieking sound beneath her. It was Claire. They were still holding on to each other.

We're both dead. Or we've fallen into some kind of space warp. The rest of the world is gone. There's just—this.

She had an impulse to touch the blue stuff, but she couldn't move because of Claire's grip on her arms. It might not have been safe anyway. Where it flowed over her, she could feel a sort of zinging and tingling as if all her blood were being excited. It smelled like the air after a storm.

And then it disappeared.

All at once. Not by stages. But it still took Jez several moments to see anything, because her eyes were blinded with dark yellow after-images. They burned and danced in front of her like a new kind of lightning, and she only gradually realized where she was.

On the train tracks. Exactly where she had been before. Except that now there was a huge, sleek BART train two feet in front of her.

She had to tilt her head to look up at its nose. It was gigantic from this angle, a monster of white, like the iceberg that sank the *Titanic*. And it was stopped dead, looking as if it had always been here, like some mountainous landmark. As if it had never moved an inch in its history.

People were yelling.

Shrieking and yowling and making all kinds of noise. It seemed to come from far away, but when Jez looked she could see them staring down at her. They were at the edge of the platform, waving their arms hysterically. As Jez stared back at them, a couple jumped down to the tracks.

Jez looked down at her cousin.

Claire was dragging in huge breaths, hyperventilating, her whole body shaking in spasms. She was staring at the train that loomed over them with eyes that showed white all around.

A loudspeaker was booming. One of the people who had jumped, a man in a security guard's uniform, was jabbering at Jez. She couldn't understand a word he was saying.

"Claire, we've got to go now."

Her cousin just whooped in air, sobbing.

"Claire, we have to *go* now. Come on." Jez's whole body felt light and strange, and when she tried to move she felt as if she were floating. But she *could* move. She stood up and pulled Claire with her.

She realized that somebody was calling her name.

It was the other person who had jumped to the tracks. It was Hugh. He was reaching for her. His gray eyes were as wide as Claire's, but not wide and hysterical. Wide and still. He was the only calm person in the crowd, beside Jez.

"Come on. Up this way," he said.

He helped her boost Claire to the platform, and then Jez scrambled up and reached down to help him. When they were all up, Jez glanced around. She knew she was looking for something—yes. There. The werewolves she'd knocked out. It seemed a hundred years ago, but they were still lying there.

"The other guy got away," Hugh said.

"Then we have to get out of here fast." Jez heard her own voice, sounding quiet and faraway. But she was beginning to feel more attached to her body. Hugh was guiding Claire toward the escalator. Jez got on the other side of Claire, and they both helped keep her on her feet.

The security guy was behind them, yelling. Jez still couldn't understand him and ignored him completely. When they reached the lower level, she and Hugh began to walk faster, pulling Claire along with them. They shoved Claire through the handicapped gate by the ticket window and vaulted over themselves.

From down here, Jez could see that the train was smoking all along its bottom. White smoke that sizzled up into the muggy air.

"We can't go on the street," Hugh said. "They've got cars out there."

"The garage," Jez said.

They both headed for it, a multistory brick building that looked dark and cool inside. They were almost running with Claire, now, and they didn't stop until they were deep within the bowels of the garage, with emptiness echoing all around them.

Then Jez sagged against a brick pillar. Hugh bent over with his hands on his knees. Claire simply folded to the ground like a marionette with all its strings cut.

Jez let herself breathe for a few minutes, let her brain settle down, before slowly lowering herself beside her cousin.

They all looked as if they'd been in an accident. Hugh's shirt was ripped and there was drying blood all down one side of his face. Claire's hair was wildly disheveled, and there were scrapes and small cuts on her face and arms. Jez herself had lost a lot of skin to the tracks, and her forearms were bleeding where Claire had scratched her.

But they were alive. Beyond all hope, they were alive.

Claire looked up just then to find Jez gazing at her. They sat for several moments simply staring into each other's eyes. Then Jez reached out to touch her cousin's cheek.

"It was you," she whispered. "All that time—and it was *you*."

She looked up at Hugh and began to laugh.

He looked back, his face pale in the semidark-ness. He shook his head and began to laugh, too, but shakily.

"Oh, Goddess," he said. "I thought you were dead, there, Jez. I thought I'd lost you."

"Not while she's around, apparently," Jez said, and laughed harder. She was slightly hysterical, but she didn't care.

Hugh's laughter sounded a little like crying. "I saw that train—and there was no way it was going to stop in time. And then—that light. It just shot out—and the train hit it. It was like a physical thing. Like a giant cushion. The train hit it and it squashed and the train went slower and then it kept squashing—"

Jez stopped laughing. "I wonder if the people on the train got hurt."

"I don't know." Hugh was sober now, too. "They must've gotten thrown around. It stopped so fast. But it didn't *smash*. They're probably okay."

"I just—from the inside, it looked like light-ning—"

"From the outside, too. I didn't imagine it would look like that—"

"I didn't know it would be so *powerful*. And, think about it; she's untrained—"

There they were, an Old Soul and a vampire hunter who'd seen everything the streets had to offer, babbling like a couple of kids.

It was Claire who stopped them. She had been looking from one of them to the other, getting more and more agitated. Now she grabbed Jez's arm.

"What are you guys *talking* about?"

Jez turned to her. She glanced at Hugh, then spoke gently.

"We're talking about you, Claire. You're the Wild Power."

CHAPTER

16

I am *not*," Claire said.

"Yeah, you are," Jez said, still gently, as if humoring a child.

"I am *not*."

"You don't even know what it is." Jez looked at Hugh. "You know what? I just realized something. The Wild Powers are all supposed to be 'born in the year of the blind Maiden's vision,' right?"

"Yeah . . ."

"Well, I was trying to figure that out all yesterday. And now, it just came to me, like *that*." She snapped her fingers. "I was thinking about visions like prophecies, you know? But I think what it meant was vision, like sight. Eyesight. Aradia only had her eyesight for a year—and *that's* the year. Seventeen years ago."

Hugh looked at Claire. "And she's—"

"Seventeen."

"So what?" Claire yelled. "So are you! So are lots of people!"

"So am I," Hugh said with a wry smile. "But not everybody can stop a train with blue fire."

"I didn't stop anything," Claire said with passionate intensity. "I don't know what a Wild Power is, but *I didn't do anything* back there. I was just lying there and I knew we were going to die—"

"And then the blue light came and the train stopped," Jez said. "You see?"

Claire shook her head. Hugh frowned and looked suddenly doubtful.

"But, Jez—what about the fire at the Marina? Claire wasn't there, was she?"

"No. But she was watching it live on TV. And she was very, very upset about it. I've still got the scars."

Hugh drew in a slow breath. His eyes were unfocused. "And you think it works across that distance?"

"I don't know. I don't see why it shouldn't." They were talking around Claire again, Jez gazing into the depths of the garage. "I think maybe distance is irrelevant to it. I think what happens is that she sees something, and if she's upset enough about it, if she's desperate enough and there's no physical way to do anything, she just—sends out the Power."

"It's completely unconscious, then," Hugh said.

"And who knows, maybe she's done it before."

Jez straightened, excited. "If it's happening far away, and she doesn't *see* the flash, and she doesn't feel anything . . ." She turned on Claire. "You didn't feel anything when you stopped the train?"

"I didn't stop the train," Claire said, slowly and with shaky patience. "And I didn't do anything about that fire at the Marina, if that's what you're talking about."

"Claire, why are you in such total denial about this?"

"Because it's not the truth. I *know* I didn't do anything, Jez. When you know, you know."

"Actually, I don't blame her," Hugh said. "It's not a great job."

Jez blinked, and then the truth swept over her. Her entire body went cold.

Oh, Goddess . . . *Claire.*

Claire's life as a normal person was over. She was going to have to leave everything, her family, her friends, and go into hiding. From this point on, she would be one of the four most important people in the world—the *only* of the four Wild Powers who was identified.

Constantly hunted. Constantly in danger. Sought after by everyone in the Night World, for a hundred different reasons.

And Claire had no experience. She was so innocent. How was she supposed to adjust to a life like that?

Jez shut her eyes. Her knees were so weak that she had to sit down.

"Oh, Claire . . . I'm sorry."

Claire gulped, staring at her. There was fear in her dark eyes.

Hugh knelt. His expression was still and sad. "I'm sorry, too," he said, speaking directly to Claire. "I don't blame you at all for not wanting this. But for right now, I think we'd better think about getting you someplace safe."

Claire now had the look of somebody after an earthquake. *How could this happen to me? Why wasn't I paying attention before it hit?*

"I . . . have to go home," she said. But she said it very slowly, looking at Jez in fear.

Jez shook her head. "Claire—you can't. I—" She paused to gather herself, then spoke quietly and firmly. "Home isn't safe anymore. There are going to be people looking for you—bad people." She glanced at Hugh.

He nodded. "A werewolf tried to run me down with a car, then jumped me. I think he must have followed me from the station. I knocked him out, but I didn't kill him."

"And there's the vampire from the platform," Jez said. "He got away—did he see the flash?"

"He saw everything. We were both right there, looking down at you. After that, he took off running. I'm sure he's going back to report to whoever sent him."

"And they'll be putting everything they have on the streets, looking for us." Jez looked around the garage. "We need transportation, Hugh."

Hugh gave a tiny grin. "Why do I have the feeling you don't mean a taxi?"

"If you've got a pocketknife, I can hotwire a car. But we have to make sure nobody's around. The last thing we need is the police."

They both stood up, Jez reaching down absent-mindedly to pull Claire to her feet.

Claire whispered, "Wait. I'm not ready for this—"

Jez braced herself to be merciless. "You're never going to be ready, Claire. Nobody is. But you have no idea what these people will do to you if they find you. You . . . just have no idea."

She located a Mustang across the garage. "That's a good one. Let's go."

There was a loose brick in the wall near the car. Jez wrapped it in her jacket and broke the window.

It only took a moment to get the door open and another few seconds to start the car. And then everybody was inside and Jez was pulling smoothly out.

"Take Ygnacio Boulevard to the freeway," Hugh said. "We've got to head south. There's a safe house in Fremont."

But they never made it out of the garage.

Jez saw the Volvo as she turned the first corner toward the exit. It had its brights on and it was heading right for them. She twisted the wheel, trying to maneuver, but a Mustang wasn't a motorcycle. She didn't have room. She couldn't slip out and get away.

The Volvo never even slowed down. And this time there was no blue light. There was a terrible crashing of metal on metal, and Jez fell into darkness.

*　　*　　*

Everything hurt.

Jez woke up slowly. For a long moment she had no idea where she was. Someplace—moving.

She was being jolted and jarred, and that wasn't good, because she seemed to be bruised all over. Now, how had that happened . . . ?

She remembered.

And sat up so fast that it made her head spin. She found herself looking around the dim interior of a van.

Dim because there were no real windows. The one in back had been covered from the outside with duct tape, and only a little light came through at the top and bottom. No light came from the front. The driver's compartment was closed off from the back by a metal wall.

There were no seats in back, nothing at all to work with. Only three figures lying motionless on the floor.

Claire. Hugh. And . . . Morgead.

Jez stared, crawling forward to look at each of them.

Claire looked all right. She had been in the backseat with a seat belt on. Her face was very pale, but she didn't seem to be bleeding and she was breathing evenly.

Hugh looked worse. His right arm was twisted oddly under him. Jez touched it gently and determined that it was broken.

And I don't have anything to set it with. And I think something else is wrong with him—his breathing's raspy.

Finally she looked at Morgead.

He looked great. He wasn't scraped or bruised or cut like the rest of them. The only injury she could find was a huge lump on his forehead.

Even as she brushed his hair back from it, he stirred.

His eyes opened and Jez found herself looking into dark emeralds.

"Jez!" He sat up, too fast. She pushed him back down. He struggled up again.

"Jez, what happened? Where are we?"

"I was hoping you might tell me that."

He was looking around the van, catching up fast. Like any vampire, he didn't stay groggy long.

"I got hit. With wood. Somebody got me when I left my apartment." He looked at her sharply. "Are you okay?"

"Yeah. I got hit with a car. But it could be worse; it was almost a train."

They were both looking around now, automatically in synch, searching for clues to their situation and ways to get out. They didn't have to discuss it. The first order of business was always escape.

"Do you have any idea who hit you?" Jez said, running her fingers over the back door. No handles, no way to get out.

"No. Pierce called to say he'd come up with something on the Wild Power. I was going to meet him when suddenly I got attacked from behind." He was going over the metal barrier that separated them from the driver's cabin, but now he glanced at her. "What do you mean, it was almost a train?"

"Nothing here. Nothing on the sides. This van is stripped."

"Nothing here, either. What do you mean, a train?"

Jez wiggled around to face him. "You really don't know?"

He stared at her for a moment. Either he was a fantastic actor, or he was both innocent and outraged. "You think *I* would do something to hurt you?"

Jez shrugged. "It's happened in the past."

He glared, seemed about to get into one of his Excited States. Then he shook his head. "I have no idea what's going on. And I would not try to hurt you."

"Then we're both in trouble."

He leaned back against the metal wall. "I believe you there." He was silent for a moment, then said in an odd, deliberate tone, "It's the Council, isn't it? They found out about Hunter's deal with us, and they're moving in."

Jez opened her mouth, shut it. Opened it again.

"Probably," she said.

She needed Morgead. Claire and Hugh weren't fighters. And whoever had them was a formidable enemy.

She didn't think it was the Council. The Council wouldn't use hired thugs; it would work through the Elders in San Francisco. And it would have no reason to kidnap Morgead; the deal with Hunter Redfern didn't really exist.

Whoever it really was had a good intelligence system, good enough to discover that Morgead knew something about the Wild Power. And had a lot of money, because it had imported a lot of muscle. And had a sense of strategy, because the kidnappings of Jez and Claire and Hugh and Morgead had been beautifully timed and nicely executed.

It might be some rogue vampire or werewolf chieftain who wanted to grab power. It might be some rival vampire gang in California. For all Jez knew, it might even be some insane faction of Circle Daybreak. The only thing that was certain was that she was going to have to fight them whenever this van got where it was going, and that she needed all the help she could get.

So it was important to lie to Morgead one last time, and hope that he would fight with her.

She had to get Claire away safely.

That was all that mattered. The world would survive without her and Morgead, and even without Hugh, although it would be a darker place. But it wouldn't survive without Claire.

"Whether it's the Council or not, we're going to have to fight them," she said out loud. "How's your energy-blast trick? The one you demonstrated when we were stick-fighting."

He snorted. "Not good. I used up all my Power fighting the guys who tackled me. It'll be a long time before I recharge."

Jez's heart sank. "Too bad," she said unemotionally. "Because those two aren't going to be able to do much."

"Those humans? Who are they, by the way?" His voice was so carefully careless again.

Jez hesitated. If she said they were unimportant, he might not help her save them. But she couldn't tell the truth, either.

"That's Claire, and this is Hugh. They're—acquaintances. They've helped me in the past."

"Humans?"

"Even humans can be useful sometimes."

"I thought maybe one of them might be the Wild Power."

"You thought if I found the Wild Power I wouldn't tell you?"

"It occurred to me."

"You're so cynical, Morgead."

"I prefer to call it observant," he said. "For instance, I can tell you something about your friend Hugh, there. I saw him in the city, just once, but I remember his face. He's a damned Daybreaker."

Jez felt a tension in her chest, but she kept her face expressionless. "So maybe I'm using him for something."

"And maybe," Morgead said, simply and pleasantly, "you're using me."

Jez lost her breath. She stared at him. His face was shadowed, but she could see its clean lines, the strong but delicate features, the darkness of his eyebrows and the tension in his jaw. And she knew, as he narrowed his eyes, that they were the color of glacier ice.

"You know," he said, "there's still a connection between us. I can feel it, sort of like a cord between our minds. It pulls. You can't deny it, Jez. It's there whether you like it or not. And—" He considered, as if thinking of the best way to put this. "It tells me things. Things about you."

Oh, hell, Jez thought. It's over. I'm just going to have to protect Hugh and Claire myself. From him and whoever's got us.

Part of her was scared, but part was just furious, the familiar fury of needing to bash Morgead over the head. He was so certain of himself, so . . . smug.

"So what's it telling you now?" she said sarcastically before she could stop herself.

"That you're not telling the truth. That there's something you're keeping from me, something you've been keeping from me. And that it has to do with him." He nodded toward Hugh.

He knew. The jerk knew and he was just playing with her. Jez could feel self-control slipping away.

"Something to do with why you want the Wild Power," Morgead went on, a strange smile playing on his lips. "And with where you've been for the past year, and with why you suddenly want to protect humans. And why you say 'Goddess' when you're surprised. No vampire says that. It's a witch thing."

Goddess, I'm going to kill him, Jez thought, clenching her teeth. "Anything else?" she said evenly.

"And with why you're scared of me reading your thoughts." He smirked. "Told you I was observant."

Jez lost it. "Yeah, Morgead, you're brilliant. So

are you smart enough to figure out what it all means? Or just to get suspicious?"

"It means—" He looked uncertain suddenly, as if he *hadn't* exactly figured out where all this was leading. He frowned. "It means . . . that you're . . ." He looked at her. "With Circle Daybreak."

It came out as a statement, but a weak one. Almost a question. And he was staring at her with an I-don't-believe-it look.

"Very good," Jez said nastily. "Two points. No, one; it took you long enough."

Morgead stared at her. Then he suddenly erupted out of his side of the van. Jez jumped forward, too, in a crouch that would let her move fluidly and protect Hugh and Claire.

But Morgead didn't attack. He just tried to grab her shoulders and shake her.

"You little *idiot!*" he yelled.

Jez was startled. "What?"

"You're a *Daybreaker?*"

"I thought you had it all figured out." What was wrong with him? Instead of looking betrayed and bloodthirsty he looked scared and angry. Like a mother whose kid has just run in front of a bus.

"I did—I guess—but I still can't *believe* it. Jez, why? Don't you know how stupid that is? Don't you realize what's going to happen to them?"

"Look, Morgead—"

"They're going to *lose*, Jez. It's not just going to be the Council against them now. Everybody in the Night World is going to be gunning for them.

They're going to get wiped out, and anybody who sides with them will be wiped out, too."

His face was two inches from hers. Jez glared at him, refusing to give ground. "I'm not just siding with them," she hissed. "I *am* one of them. I'm a damned Daybreaker."

"You're a dead Daybreaker. I can't believe this. How am I supposed to protect you from the whole Night World?"

She stared at him. *"What?"*

He settled back, glaring, but not at her. He was looking around the van, avoiding her eyes. "You heard me. I don't care who your friends are, Jez. I don't even care that you came back to use me. I'm just glad you came back. We're soulmates, and nothing can change that." Then he shook his head furiously. "Even if you won't admit it."

"Morgead . . ." Suddenly the ache in Jez's chest was too much to stay inside. It was closing off her throat, making her eyes sting, trying to make her cry.

She had misjudged Morgead, too. She'd been so sure that he would hate her, that he could never forgive.

But of course, he didn't know the whole truth yet.

He probably thought that her being a Daybreaker was something she would grow out of. That it was just a matter of getting her to see the light and change sides again, and she would become the old Jez Redfern. He didn't realize that the old Jez Redfern had been an illusion.

"I'm sorry," she said abruptly, helplessly. "For all of this, Morgead—I'm sorry. It really wasn't fair to you for me to come back."

He looked irritated. "I told you; I'm glad you did. We can work things out—if you'll just stop being so *stubborn*. We'll get out of this—"

"Even if we do get out of it, nothing's going to change." She looked up at him. She wasn't frightened of what he might do anymore. The only thing she was frightened of was seeing disgust in his eyes—but she still had to tell him. "I can't be your soulmate, Morgead."

He hardly seemed to be listening to her. "Yes, you can. I told you, I don't care who your friends are. We'll keep you alive somehow. The only thing I don't understand is why you'd *want* to ally yourself with stupid humans, when you know they're going to lose."

Jez looked at him. Morgead, the vampire's vampire, whose only interest was in seeing the Night World conquer humanity completely. Who was what she had been a year ago, and what she could never be again. Who thought of her as an ally, a descendent of one of the first families of the lamia.

Who thought he loved who he thought she was.

Jez kept looking at him steadily, and when she spoke, it was very quietly. And it was the truth.

"Because *I'm* a human," she said.

CHAPTER

17

Morgead's entire body jerked once and then went absolutely still. As if he'd been turned to stone. The only thing alive about him was his eyes, which were staring at Jez with shock and burning disbelief.

Well, Jez told herself, with a grim humor that was almost like sobbing grief, I startled him, that's for sure. I finally managed to stun Morgead speechless.

It was only then that she realized some part of her had hoped that he already knew this, too. That he would be able to brush it off with exasperation, the way he had the fact that she was a Daybreaker.

But that hope was shattered now. It had been a stupid hope anyway. Being a Daybreaker was something that could change, a matter of confused attitude.

Being vermin was permanent.

"But that's—that's not—" Morgead seemed to be having trouble getting the words out. His eyes were large with horror and denial. "That's not *possible*. You're a vampire."

"Only half," Jez said. She felt as if she were killing something—and she was. She was murdering any hope for what was between them.

Might as well stomp it good, she thought bitterly. She couldn't understand the wetness that was threatening to spill out of her eyes.

"The other half is human," she said shortly, almost viciously. "My mother was human. Claire is my cousin, and she's human. I've been living with my uncle Jim, my mother's brother, and his family. They're all human."

Morgead shut his eyes. A moment of astonishing weakness for him, Jez thought coldly.

His voice was still a whisper. "Vampires and humans can't have kids. You can't be half and half."

"Oh, yeah, I can. My father broke the laws of the Night World. He fell in love with a human, and they got married, and here I am. And then, when I was three or so, some other vampires came and tried to kill us all." In her mind Jez was seeing it again, the woman with red hair who looked like a medieval princess, begging for her child's life. The tall man trying to protect her. "*They* knew I was half human. They kept yelling 'Kill the freak.' So that's what I am, you see." She turned eyes she knew were feverishly bright on him. "A freak."

He was shaking his head, gulping as if he were

about to be sick. It made Jez hate him, and feel sorry for him at the same time. She scarcely noticed that hot tears were spilling down her cheeks.

"I'm vermin, Morgead. One of *them*. Prey. That's what I realized a year ago, when I left the gang. Up until then I had no idea, but that last night we hunted, I remembered the truth. And I knew that I had to go away and try to make up for all the things I'd done to humans."

He put a hand up to press against his eyes.

"I didn't just become a Daybreaker. I became a vampire hunter. I track down vampires who like to kill, who enjoy making humans suffer, and I stake them. You know why? Because they deserve to die."

He was looking at her again, but as if he could hardly stand to. "Jez—"

"It's weird. I don't know about our *connection*"— she smiled bitterly at him, to let him know she knew all that was over now—"but I felt bad lying to you. I'm almost glad to finally tell you the truth. I kind of wanted to tell you a year ago when it happened, but I knew you'd kill me, and that made me a little hesitant."

She was laughing now. She realized she was more than a little hysterical. But it didn't seem to matter. Nothing mattered while Morgead was looking at her with that sick disbelief in his eyes.

"So, anyway . . ." She stretched her muscles, still smiling at him, but ready to defend herself. "Are you going to try and kill me now? Or is the engagement just off?"

He simply looked at her. It was as if his entire spirit had gone out of him. He didn't speak, and all at once Jez couldn't think of anything to say, either. The silence stretched and stretched, like a yawning chasm between them.

They were so far away from each other.

You knew all along it would come to this, Jez's mind told her mockingly. How can you presume to be upset? He's actually taking it better than you expected. He hasn't tried to tear your throat out yet.

At last Morgead said, in a flat and empty voice, "That's why you wouldn't drink my blood."

"I haven't had a blood meal for a year," Jez said, feeling equally empty. "I don't need to, if I don't use my Powers."

He stared past her at the metal wall. "Well, maybe you'd better drink some of your human friends'," he said tiredly. "Because whoever has us—"

He broke off, suddenly alert. Jez knew what it was. The van was slowing down, and the tires were crunching on gravel.

They were pulling into a driveway.

A long driveway, and a steep one. We're somewhere out in the country, Jez thought.

She didn't have time for any more banter with Morgead. Although she felt drained and numb, she was focused on outside issues now.

"Look," she said tensely as the van braked. "I know you hate me now, but whoever has us hates us both. I'm not asking you to help me. I just want to get my cousin away—and I'm asking you not to stop me from doing that. Later, you can fight me or whatever. We can take care of that between the two of us. Just don't stop me from saving Claire."

He just looked at her with dark and hollow eyes. He didn't agree or disagree. He didn't move when she positioned herself to erupt out of the van as soon as the back door was opened.

But, as it turned out, she could have saved her breath. Because when the door did open, letting in sunlight that blinded Jez, it was to reveal five vicious-looking thugs, completely blocking the entrance. Three of them had spears with deadly points leveled right at Jez. The other two had guns.

"If anybody tries to fight," a voice from around the side of the van said, "shoot the unconscious ones in the kneecaps."

Jez sagged back. She didn't try to fight as they forced her out of the van.

Neither, strangely, did Morgead. There were more thugs standing around behind the van, enough to surround both Jez and Morgead with a forest of spears as they were led to the house.

It was a nice house, a small sturdy Queen Anne painted barn red. There were trees all around and no other buildings in sight.

We're out in the boondocks, Jez thought. Maybe Point Reyes Park. Somewhere remote, anyway, where nobody can hear us scream.

They were shepherded into the living room of the house, and Hugh and Claire were dumped unceremoniously on the floor.

And then they were all tied up.

Jez kept watching for an opportunity to attack. But one never came. All the time she and Morgead were being tied, two of the thugs pointed guns at Claire and Hugh. There was no way Jez could disarm them both before they got off a shot.

Worse, she was being rendered helpless by an expert. The cords were made of bast, the inner bark of trees. Equally effective against vampires and humans. When the guy tying her up was through, she had no use of her arms or legs.

Hugh woke up, gasping with pain, when they tied his injured arm. Claire woke up when the werewolf thug who'd finished winding cords around her slapped her.

Jez looked at that particular 'wolf carefully. She was too angry to glare at him. But she wanted to remember his face.

Then she looked back at Claire, who was staring around her in bewilderment.

"I—where are we? What's going on, Jez?"

Hugh was also looking around, but with much less confusion. His gray eyes were simply sad and full of pain.

"It's all right, Claire," Jez said. "Just keep quiet, okay? We're in a little trouble, but don't tell them anything." She stared at her cousin, trying to will her to understand.

"A little trouble? I don't think so," came a voice from the living room doorway.

It was the same voice that had given the order

about shooting kneecaps. A light, cold voice, like an Arctic wind.

The speaker was a girl.

A very pretty girl, Jez thought irrelevantly. She had black hair that fell straight down her back like silk, and eyes that gleamed like topaz. Porcelain skin. A cruel smile. Lots of Power that surrounded her like a dark aura.

A vampire.

She looked perhaps a year older than Jez, but that didn't mean anything. She could be any age.

And those eyes, Jez thought. They're vaguely familiar. Like something I've seen in a picture. . . .

"I should probably introduce myself," the girl said, looking at her with cold mockery. "I'm Lily Redfern."

Jez felt her stomach plummet.

Hunter Redfern's daughter.

Well, that explained a lot.

She was working for her father, of course. And she was a powerful enemy herself, over four hundred years old. There were rumors that last year she'd been working the human slave trade, and making a lot of money at it.

I should laugh, Jez thought. There I was telling Morgead that Hunter wanted to steal a march on the Council—and here he really did. Just not through me, of course. He's sent his only surviving child out to take care of us, to get Morgead to turn over the Wild Power.

And that's why so many thugs—he can afford to buy as many as he needs. And the smooth operation—Lily's a born strategist. Not to mention absolutely merciless and cold as ice.

She was right. We're not in a little trouble. We're in a whole lot.

Somebody, Jez thought with a strange, quiet certainty, *is going to die here.*

Lily was still talking. "And now let me introduce my associates, who've done so much to make this all possible." She gestured at someone hidden in the hall to come forward. "This is Azarius. I think you've met."

It was the vampire Jez had fought on the platform. He was tall, with dark skin and a look of authority.

"And this," Lily said, smiling, "is someone you've also met." She gestured again, and a second figure appeared in the doorway.

It was Pierce Holt.

He was smiling faintly, his aristocratic face drawn in lines of genteel triumph. He waved one slender hand at them, his eyes as cold as Lily's.

Morgead gave an inarticulate roar and tried to lunge at him.

He only succeeded in falling on the floor, a struggling body in a cocoon of bast. Lily and Azarius both laughed. Pierce just looked scornful.

"You really didn't guess?" he said. "You're so stupid, Morgead. Coming out this morning to meet me, so trusting, so naive—I thought you were smarter. I'm disappointed."

"No, you're *dead*," Morgead raged from the floor. He was staring at Pierce, black hair falling over his forehead and into green eyes that were blazing with rage. "You are *dead* when this is over! You betrayed the gang. You're complete scum. You're—"

"Shut him up," Lily said, and one of the thugs kicked Morgead in the head.

He must really be out of power, Jez thought, wincing. Or he'd have blasted Pierce then.

"I'm smart," Pierce was saying. "And I'm going to survive. I knew something was fishy when *she*"—he nodded toward Jez without looking at her—"said she had a deal with Hunter Redfern. It didn't sound right—and then the way she was *so* worried about that vermin kid. So I made a few calls, and I found out the truth."

"You realize that your friend there is working with Circle Daybreak," Lily interrupted. She was also looking at Morgead and ignoring Jez. "She lied to you and tricked you. She was trying to get the Wild Power for them."

Morgead snarled something inarticulate.

"And she's not just a Daybreaker," Pierce said. Finally he looked at Jez, and it was with venomous spite. "She's a mutant abomination. She's half vermin. She should have been drowned at birth."

"*You* should have been drowned at birth," Morgead said through locked teeth.

Lily had been watching in amusement, but now she waved one hand. "Okay, enough fun and games. Down to business." Two of the thugs sat Morgead back up, and Lily walked to the middle of the room. She looked at each of them in turn, Jez last. "I've only got one question for you," she said in her cool, quiet voice. "Which human is the Wild Power?"

Jez stared at her.

She doesn't know. She knows almost everything else, but not that. And if she can't find out . . .

Jez gave Hugh and Claire one long, intense look, telling them to keep silent. Then she looked back at Lily.

"I have no idea what you're talking about."

Lily hit her.

It was a pretty good blow, but nothing to compare with what Jez got when she was in a fight. Jez laughed, a natural laugh of surprise and scorn.

Lily's hawklike golden eyes went icy.

"You think this is funny?" she said, still quietly. "My father sent me to get the Wild Power, and that's just what I'm going to do. Even if it means tearing you and your vampire boyfriend to pieces, mutant."

"Yeah, well, suppose I don't know? Did you ever think of that? Then I *can't* tell, no matter what you and your little . . ." Jez glanced at Pierce and Azarius. "Your little hobgoblins do."

Lily's porcelain skin was flushing with fury. It brought out faint scars on one side of her face that Jez hadn't noticed before, like mostly-healed burn marks. "Look, you little freak—" Then she turned to the thugs. "Teach her a lesson."

Things were exciting for a while. Jez could hear Claire and Hugh yelling and Morgead snarling while the hobgoblins beat her up. She hardly felt the blows herself. She was in a place where they didn't matter.

When they finally got tired and stopped, Lily walked up to her again.

"Now," she said sweetly, "has your memory gotten any better."

Jez looked at her from under a swelling eyelid. "I can't tell you something I don't know."

Lily opened her mouth, but before she could speak, a new voice cut in.

"She doesn't have to tell you," Hugh said. "I'll tell you. It's me."

Lily swiveled slowly to look at him.

He was sitting up straight inside his cocoon of bonds, his face calm under the dried blood. His gray eyes were clear and straightforward. He didn't look afraid.

Oh, Hugh, Jez thought. Her heart was beating slow and hard and her eyes prickled.

Lily glanced at Azarius.

He shrugged. "Sure, it could be. I told you, it could be either of them. They were both at the station when the flash came and the train stopped."

"Hmm," Lily said, a sound like a cat purring to dinner. She moved toward Hugh. He didn't look away from her, didn't flinch.

But beside him, Claire gave a convulsive wiggle.

She had been watching everything with a desperate, dazed expression. Jez was sure she didn't understand a quarter of what was going on. But now she suddenly lost the muddled look. Her dark eyes sparked and she looked like the Claire who'd taunted Jez a hundred times in the hallway back home.

"I don't know *what* you're talking about," she said to Hugh. "You know perfectly well it's me." She turned to Lily. "I'm the Wild Power."

Lily's mouth tightened. She put her hands on her hips, looking from Hugh to Claire.

Then Jez heard the strangest sound of her life.

It was laughing—a wild and reckless laughing. There was an edge almost like crying to it, but also something that was exhilarated, daredevil, free.

"If you *really* want to know who it is," Morgead said, "it's *me*."

Lily whirled to glare at him. Jez simply stared, dumbfounded.

She'd never seen him look so handsome—or so mocking. His smile was brilliant and flashing, his dark hair was falling all over his eyes, and his eyes were blazing green emeralds. He was tied up, but he was sitting with his head thrown back like a prince.

Something tore inside Jez.

She didn't understand why he would do it. He must know he wasn't saving her. The only people he might possibly save were Hugh and Claire. And why would he care about them?

Besides, it was a futile gesture. He didn't realize that he *couldn't* be the Wild Power, that he hadn't been around when the train stopped.

But—it was such a gallant gesture, too. Probably the most gallant thing Jez had ever seen.

She stared at him, feeling the wetness spill from

her eyes again, wishing she were telepathic and could ask him why in the worlds he had done it.

Then his green eyes turned to her, and she heard his mental voice.

There's just a chance they'll let one of them go with a beating. Just maybe—as a warning to Circle Daybreak not to mess with Hunter anymore. Especially if I convince Lily I'll work with her.

Jez couldn't answer, but she shook her head very faintly, and looked at him in despair. She knew he could read that. *Do you know what they'll do to* you? *Especially when they find out you're a fake?*

She saw his faint answering smile. He knew.

What difference does it make? he said in her mind. *You and me—we're lost anyway. And without you, I don't care what happens.*

Jez couldn't show any reaction to that at all. Her vision was dimming, and her heart felt as if it were trying to claw itself out of her chest.

Oh, Morgead . . .

Lily was breathing hard, on the verge of losing control. "If I have to kill all of you—"

"Wait," Pierce said, his cool voice a striking contrast to Lily's strained one. "There's a simple way to find out." He pointed at Jez. "Stake her."

Lily glared at him. *"What?"*

"She's never going to tell you anything. She's expendable. And there's something you have to understand about the Wild Power." He moved smoothly to Lily's side. "I think Morgead was right about one thing. I think the Wild Power isn't operating consciously at this point. It's only when the danger is greatest, when there's no physical way to escape, that the power comes out."

Lily cast a sideways look at Hugh and Claire, who were sitting tensely, their eyes wide. "You mean *they* may not know which it is?"

"Maybe not. Maybe it's completely automatic at this point. But there's one way to find out. They all seem—attached—to the halfbreed. Put her life in danger, and then see which of them can break free and try to save her."

Lily's perfect lips slowly curved in a smile. "I knew there was a reason I liked you," she said.

Then she gestured at the thugs. "Go on, do it."

Everything was confused for a bit. Not because Jez was struggling. She wasn't. But Claire was screaming and Hugh and Morgead were shouting, and Lily was laughing. When the worst of the noise died down, Jez found herself on her back. Azarius was standing over her, and he was holding a hammer and stake.

"Isn't it interesting," Lily was saying, "that a stake through the heart is the one thing that takes care of humans and vampires equally efficiently?"

"And halfbreeds, too," Pierce said. They were on either side of Azarius, looking down and laughing.

"Lily, listen. *Listen*," Morgead said, his voice hoarse and desperate. "You don't have to do this. I already told you, it's me. Just wait a minute and *talk* to me—"

"Don't even bother, human-lover," Lily said without glancing at him. "If you're the Wild Power, then save her."

"Don't any of you do anything!" Jez yelled. "Not *anything*, do you understand?"

She was yelling it mainly at Claire—or was she? Suddenly Jez felt strangely uncertain.

Her heart was beating very quickly, and her mind was racing even faster. Fragments of thought were glittering through her consciousness, like bits of melody almost too faint to catch. It was as if all the prophecies she'd heard about the Wild Powers were echoing, ricocheting around her brain at insane speed. And there was something about them, something that was bothering her. Something that made her wonder . . .

Could it be that Claire *wasn't* the Wild Power? Jez had assumed she was—but was it possible that she'd been wrong?

Hugh had been on the platform, too, watching the train approach. Hugh had reason to be upset at having to watch Jez die. He cared about her. Jez knew that now. And Hugh was seventeen.

Could Hugh be the Wild Power?

He hadn't been in the Marina district—but he lived in the Bay Area; there was no reason he couldn't have been watching the fire just as she and Claire had.

But there was still something nagging at her. The prophecies . . . 'two eyes are watching' . . . 'Four of blue fire, power in their blood. . . .'

Lily was speaking. Jez heard her as if from a great distance.

"Do it. Right beside the heart first."

Azarius positioned the stake. He raised the hammer.

Morgead screamed, *"Jez!"*

Jez shouted, "None of you do anything—"

And then the hammer came down and the universe exploded in red agony.

CHAPTER

Jez heard herself scream, but only faintly.

There was a roaring in her ears as if the BART train was coming at her again. And a pain that engulfed her whole body, sending agonized spasms through her limbs. It centered in her chest, though, where something white-hot was lodged inside her, crushing her lung and dislodging her internal organs and burning right beside her heart.

She'd been staked.

What she had done so often to others had been done to her.

She hadn't realized anything could hurt like this. She was glad none of her victims had lived long to keep suffering.

The wood of the stake was poisoning her heart, she knew. Even if it were removed, she would die.

No vampire could survive contact between living wood and its undead heart.

Still, she would live for a little while—in unimaginable agony as the poison ate through her.

A voice was screaming in her mind. *JezJezJezJez* . . . Over and over, incoherently.

Morgead, she thought. And she hoped he wasn't feeling any of what she was feeling through the silver cord that connected them.

Hugh and Claire were sobbing. Jez wished they wouldn't. They had to stay calm; to think of a way to save themselves.

Because she couldn't help them anymore.

Over the sobbing she heard a shrill and angry voice. Lily.

"What is wrong with you?" Lily was saying. "Don't you see what's happening to her? Don't you *want* to save her?"

Through the red haze that filled Jez's vision, she felt dim approval. They were doing what she'd told them. Whichever of them was the Wild Power was suppressing it.

Good. That was what mattered. Although she couldn't really remember why any longer. . . .

Suddenly a face broke through the red haze. It was Lily, bending over her.

"Don't *you* understand?" Lily yelled. "You can stop this right now. I'll have him kill you cleanly— all the pain will be over. All you have to do is tell me who it is."

Jez smiled at her faintly. She couldn't breathe to answer, and she didn't want to try.

Would you believe that I don't know? she thought. No, I don't think you would. . . .

The pain was getting less by itself. It was as if Jez was moving farther and farther away from it.

"How can you be so *stupid?*" Lily was screaming. Her face was twisted, and to Jez's vision, floating in a scarlet mist. She looked like a monster. Then she turned and seemed to be screaming at someone else. "All right. Get the other vampire down here, too. Morgead." She was looking at Jez again. "We'll just have to stake your friends one after another until the Wild Power decides to reveal itself."

No. *No* . . .

Suddenly everything was much clearer around Jez. She could see the room again, and she could feel her own body. There was still the roaring in her ears, but she could hear Claire's sobs over it.

No. Lily couldn't mean it. This couldn't be happening. . . .

But it was. They were shoving Morgead down on the floor beside her, and Claire and Hugh beyond him. The thugs with spears were getting into position.

No. No. *This can't happen.*

Jez wanted to scream at them, to tell the Wild Power to do something, because everything was lost now anyway. But she didn't have air to scream. And she felt so adrift and confused anyway. . . . Her universe had become disjointed. Her thoughts seemed to be unraveling at all once, past memories combining with flashing sensory impressions from the present, and with strange new ideas. . . .

If it was involuntary, why didn't the Wild Power work magic more often? Unless there was some other requirement. . . .

I can't let this happen.

The dampness of blood spreading around her heart. . . .

Claire's nails digging into her arms.

"When there's no physical way to escape . . ."

Power in the blood.

Claire on the floor there. Screaming and screaming . . .

Something building inside her, hotter than the stake.

Morgead beside her whispering, "Jez, I love you."

Pierce with the stake over him. Morgead looking up unafraid. . . .

Hotter than the heart of a star.

Hugh in the distance saying almost quietly, "Goddess of Life, receive us; guide us to the other world. . . ."

Hotter than the sun and colder and bluer than the moon, like fire that burned and froze and crackled like lightning all at once. Something that filled her with an energy that was past rage and past love and past all controlling and that she recognized in her soul even though she'd never consciously felt it before. It was swelling Jez to bursting, a pure and terrible flame that was never meant to be unleashed like this. . . .

"Do it!" Lily shouted.

And Jez let it free.

It came roaring out from her in a silent explosion. Blue fire that streamed from her body and blasted in all directions, but especially up. It came out and out and out, engulfing everything, flowing from her in a neverending torrent. Like a solar flare that didn't stop.

It was all she could see. Blue flames, streaked with blue-white lightning that crackled almost soundlessly. Just like the fire that had cocooned her on the BART tracks.

Except that now she could tell where it was coming from, even if she couldn't direct it. She knew how to let it out, now, but once out it did what it wanted.

And it wasn't meant to be used this way. That was the only thing she knew clearly about it. She'd been letting it slip out when she was desperately upset—when she was worried for someone's life, and she knew that she couldn't do anything else to save them. That was forgivable, because it had been unconscious.

This wasn't. She was probably violating some law of the universe or something. The blue fire was only meant to be used in the last battle, when the darkness came and the Four were called to stand against it.

I suppose that means I should try to stop now, Jez thought.

She wasn't sure how to do it. She guessed that she needed to call it back, somehow, to draw it down into her body again.

Maybe if I sort of tug. . . .

She did—something. A gathering-up with her mind. It was harder than letting the fire go had been, but it worked. She could feel it returning, flooding back inside her, as if she were sucking it in. . . .

And then it was gone, and Jez could see the world again. Could see what it had done.

The house had disappeared.

Or most of it, anyway. There was about a foot and a half of ragged wall left all around, with charred insulation spilling out. Blue energy like electricity ran along the edges here and there, fizzing.

Other than that, no house. Not even chunks of wreckage lying around. There were fine bits of debris floating down, making the sunlight hazy, but that was all.

It got . . . vaporized, Jez thought, searching for the right word.

No Lily. No Azarius. No Pierce. And none of the ugly thugs.

Goddess, Jez thought. I didn't mean to do that. I only wanted to stop them from hurting Morgead and Claire and Hugh. . . .

What about them? she thought in a sudden panic. She turned her head, painfully.

They were there. And alive. They were even stirring. The cords they'd been tied with were lying on the carpet, sizzling with that same blue energy.

It's so weird to have a carpet without a house to go with it, Jez thought fuzzily.

She was going away again. And that was too bad, but at least it didn't hurt anymore. The pain was gone completely, replaced by a warm and sleepy feeling—and the sensation of gently floating outward.

Her eyelids felt heavy.

"Jez? Jez!"

It was a husky whisper. Jez opened her eyes to see Morgead's face.

He was crying. Oh, dear, that was bad. Jez hadn't seen him cry since . . . when was it? Sometime when they'd been little kids. . . .

Jez, can you hear me? Now he was talking in her mind.

Jez blinked again, and tried to think of something comforting to say to him.

"I feel warm," she whispered.

"No, you don't!" He said it almost in a growl. Then he looked behind him, and Jez saw Hugh and Claire crawling up. They were all shining with golden light.

"You're so pretty," she told them. "Like angels."

"This isn't the time for your weird humor!" Morgead shouted.

"Stop it! Don't yell at her!" That was Claire. Claire was crying, too, lovely tears that shone as they fell. She reached out and took Jez's hand, and that was nice, although Jez couldn't exactly feel it. She could see it.

"She's going to be all right," Morgead was snarling. "She's lost blood, but she'll be okay."

Someone was stroking Jez's hair off her face. She

felt that; it was pleasant. She frowned slowly at Morgead, because there was something important to tell him, and talking was difficult.

"Tell Hugh . . ." she whispered.

"Tell Hugh your freaking self! He's right here! And you're not going anywhere."

Jez blinked with the difficulty changing focus. Yes, there was Hugh. He was the one stroking her hair.

"Hugh . . . the prophecy. I figured out what the two eyes watching were. They're the sun and the moon—get it? Two eyes . . . for somebody who belongs to both worlds."

"The Day World and the Night World," Hugh said softly. "You got it, Jez. That was so smart."

"And blood," Jez whispered. " 'Power in the blood'—that's why I couldn't do it anytime I wanted. Blood has to flow before you can let out the power. The first two times Claire was scratching me. And this time . . ." Her voice died off, but it wasn't important. Everybody could see the blood this time, she knew.

Hugh's voice was thick. "That was smart, too, Jez. You figured it out. And you saved us. You did everything just right."

"No . . . because there's only going to be three Wild Powers now. . . ."

"No, there *aren't*," Morgead raged. "Listen to me, Jez. There's no reason for you to die—"

Jez couldn't manage a smile anymore, or a sentence. But she whispered gently, "Wood . . . poison."

"No, it isn't! Not to humans. And you're half human, Jez. You're vampire enough to survive something that would kill a human, but you're human enough not to be poisoned by wood."

Jez knew better. She couldn't see much anymore. Only Morgead, and he was getting indistinct. It wasn't that the world was dimming, though—it was getting brighter. Everything was golden and shining.

Four less one and darkness triumphs, Jez thought. *I'm so sorry about that. I hope they can manage it somehow. It would be so sad for everything human to be lost. There's so much good in the world, and so much to love. . . .*

She couldn't even see Morgead now. Only gold. But she could hear. She could hear Claire whispering to her in a voice broken by tears, and feel wetness dropping on her face.

"I love you, Jez. You're the best cousin anybody could ever have."

And Hugh. He was crying, too. "Jez, I'm so proud to be your friend. . . ."

And then, through the mist and the gold and the warmth and peace, came a voice that wasn't gentle at all. That was roaring in sheer outrage and fury.

"DON'T YOU DARE DIE ON ME, JEZEBEL! DON'T YOU DARE! Or I'll follow you to the next world and KILL you."

Suddenly, in the pretty gold mist, she could see something else. The only thing in the universe that wasn't golden.

It was a silver cord.

"You come back and you do it right now," Morgead bellowed in her ears and in her mind. *"Right now! Do you hear me?"*

The peace was shattered. Nothing seemed quite so warm and wonderful anymore, and she knew that once Morgead got into one of his Excited States, he wouldn't stop yelling until he got what he wanted.

And there was the cord right in front of her. It was strong, and she could feel that the other end was somewhere in Morgead's heart, and that he was trying to drag her back to him.

All right. Maybe if I just grab on. . . .

Somehow, she was holding on to it, and bit by bit, pulling herself back. And then the golden light was fading and she was inside a body that hurt and Morgead was holding her and kissing her and crying all at the same time.

Claire's voice came from beyond him. "She's breathing again! She's breathing!"

"I love you, you stupid human," Morgead gasped against Jez's cheek. "I can't live without you. Don't you know that?"

Jez whispered, "I told you never to call me Jezebel."

Then she fainted.

"Time for a nice bath," the nurse said. "And then we can have a visitor."

Jez eyed her narrowly. The woman was kind, but she had some mania for sponge baths, and she was always putting strange-smelling ingredients in the water. Which was actually not that surprising since she was a witch.

"Skip the bath," Jez said. "Let the visitor in."

"Now, now," the witch said, shaking a finger and advancing with the sponge.

Jez sighed. Being a Wild Power in a Circle Daybreak sanctuary meant that she could have pretty much anything she wanted—except that everyone was still treating her like a little kid. Especially the nurses, who spoiled her and flattered her, but talked to her as if she were about three.

Still, she was glad to let the Circle take care of some things. Keeping her relatives safe, for instance. Although she was almost fully recovered, thanks to a strong constitution and a lot of healing spells from the witches, she wasn't up to that yet. Uncle Bracken and the entire Goddard family needed constant protection, since Hunter Redfern and the Night World Council were all undoubtedly after them by now.

The Circle had imported some experts from back East to take care of it. A rival vampire hunter, of all things, named Rashel something. Plus her soulmate, a vampire-turned-Daybreaker called Quinn.

At least they were competent. They'd gotten Jez's uncle Bracken, as well as the remnants of the gang out of San Francisco, a city that was going to be bad for their health for a while. Morgead was trying to get the gang to join Circle Daybreak for their own good, and he said that Raven, at least, was showing some interest. Val and Thistle were being stubborn, but that was hardly surprising. What was important was that they were alive.

Pierce, on the other hand, was simply gone. No one had seen a trace of him or Lily or any of her people since Jez blasted them. Apparently they had truly been vaporized, and Jez couldn't bring herself to feel *too* badly.

"All done!" the nurse said brightly, straightening Jez's pajama top. Which was just as well because at that moment a black head came poking in the door.

"What is going *on* in here? You getting ready to go to the opera or something?"

Jez raised her eyebrows at Morgead. "Maybe. Are you telling me I can't?"

He snorted and came in as the nurse went out. "I wouldn't dare tell you that. You're the princess, right? You can have anything."

"Right," Jez said, with huge satisfaction. "So how're Hugh and Claire?"

"Claire's fine; she fits right in with the witches here. I think she's trying to get them to put up a Web page. And Hugh's just his same stupid self. He's off saving chipmunks from toxic waste or something."

"And how about the kid?"

"The kid," Morgead said, "is living it up. The Daybreakers are crazy about her; something about one of the oldest Old Souls ever found—I dunno. Anyway, they're trying to talk her mom into letting her live here. She says thanks for saving her life and she's drawing you a picture."

Jez nodded, pleased. It would be nice if Iona came to live at the sanctuary; it meant Jez could see her a lot. Not that Jez planned to live here all the time herself—she and Morgead needed their freedom. They couldn't be penned in; they had to be able to come and go. She just hadn't gotten around to telling the Daybreakers that yet.

With the people she loved taken care of, she could turn her attention to other matters. "Is that chocolate?"

"It's the only reason you like to see me, isn't it?" Morgead said, allowing her to take the box. He sat beside her, looking tragic.

"Nah," Jez said with her mouth full. She swallowed. "Everybody brings 'em." Then she grinned. "I like to see you for a different reason."

He grinned wickedly back. "I can't think what that could be."

"Hmm . . . you're right . . . maybe there *is* no other reason."

"Watch it, Jezebel," he growled and leaned forward menacingly.

"Don't call me that, idiot."

"You're the idiot, idiot."

"And you're—" But Jez never got to finish, because he stopped her mouth with a kiss.

And then his arms were around her—so gently—and the silver cord was humming and everything was warm and there were only the two of them in the world.

One from the land of kings long forgotten;
One from the hearth which still holds the spark;
One from the Day World where two eyes are
    watching;
One from the twilight to be one with the dark.

ABOUT THE AUTHOR

LISA JANE SMITH is the author of more than twenty books for young adults. She is looking forward to the millennium and wonders what the future will bring. She enjoys computers, mythology, walking in the woods at night, and animals. She lives in northern California, in a rambling house among the trees, and gets some of her best ideas sitting under the stars.

Her Archway trilogies include *The Forbidden Game* and *Dark Visions*.

Don't miss the next

NIGHT WORLD™

Black Dawn

When her older brother Miles disappears, nothing is going to stop Maggie from finding him. But the trail takes her into the most secret heart of the Night World—a kingdom ruled by the young vampire Delos, where humans live as slaves. Delos and Maggie are soulmates—but will she have to destroy him to survive?

R·L·STINE'S
GHOSTS of FEAR STREET ®

- -

Simon & Schuster Mail Order
200 Old Tappan Rd., Old Tappan, N.J. 07675
Please send me the books I have checked above. I am enclosing $_____ (please add
$0.75 to cover the postage and handling for each order. Please add appropriate sales
tax). Send check or money order–no cash or C.O.D.'s please. Allow up to six weeks
for delivery. For purchase over $10.00 you may use VISA: card number, expiration
date and customer signature must be included.

POCKET
BOOKS

Name _____

Address _____

City _____ State/Zip _____

VISA Card # _____ Exp.Date _____

Signature _____

1180-24